the Great Spirit Horse

OTOKA (oh-doh-kah) - the beginning

the Great Spirit Horse

OTOKA (oh-doh-kah) - the beginning

by Linda Little Wolf

PELICAN PUBLISHING COMPANY
Gretna 2003

First published by Syncopated Press, 2001
Published by arrangement with the author by
  Pelican Publishing Company, Inc., 2003

First printing, 2001
First Pelican printing, 2003

*The word "Pelican" and the depiction of a pelican are trademarks
of Pelican Publishing Company, Inc., and are registered in the
U.S. Patent and Trademark Office.*

Library of Congress Cataloging-in-Publication Data
Wolf, Linda Little
The Great Spirit Horse / Linda Little Wolf.
      p.   cm.
          ISBN 1-58980-123-7 (pbk.)
          1. Fiction
  I. Wolf, Linda Little
  II. Title

Cover, design, and illustrations by Kimberly Graham

Printed in Canada

Published by Pelican Publishing Company, Inc.
1000 Burmaster Street, Gretna, Louisiana 70053

DEDICATED TO

Vito – my pillar of strength, loyalty, understanding and love.

My Parents – with gratitude, for giving me the ability to see dreams and the courage to make them a reality.

Leslie (Second Voice Coyote Woman) – forever my guardian spirit and my guiding light. Always in my thoughts and heart.

Brooke – a precious gift from a "Spirit Horse," my traveling companion, and my treasured friend.

Enough Stuff – my beloved blue-eyed equine inspiration. My journey began, my world changed, when your gentle spirit entered my life.

All the children – who have touched my heart with their vivid imaginations, endless curiosity, and contagious laughter. My gifts to you are my words filled with the many voices of my ancestors.

"Pilamayaye"

Linda Little Wolf

INTRODUCTION

Let me introduce myself. My name is Sunka Wakan (shoon-kah wah-kahn), the Great Spirit Horse. I guess you could say that I am a very unique animal. I was born different from most horses.

My birthplace was the Great Plains some 250 years ago. I know that makes me very old, but I have lived all these years because I have become a legend. You see, legends never die. They live on forever in the hearts of those who love to hear them. My story has been told for centuries by the nomadic tribes of Indians living on the Great Plains.

It has been brought to my attention that in recent years, humans have

expressed great interest in learning about Native American folklore. Rather than having a human being describe my life one more time, I thought it would be more fitting for you to hear my legend straight from the horse's mouth. For the very first time in history, I, Sunka Wakan, wish to tell my story to mankind.

CHAPTER ONE

I came into this world the way most horses do. My first encounter with the cold, hard ground was a frightful experience. My fears disappeared when I caught the scent of my mother and felt her warm breath on my face.

The horses from our herd gathered around, curious to see me. I was the center of attention, and loved every minute of it. But they quickly stepped aside to make way for my father, Raven, the herd leader.

Raven came forward to inspect me. I remember looking into his jet-black eyes for the first time. I expected them to be filled with the same joy I saw in my mother's face. Instead, they showed confusion and dismay. I'll never forget that, nor the conversation that followed.

"What is this, Star Face?" he said to my mother. "All these strange markings! Why is our son covered with so many spots? They are everywhere! He should be a solid-colored horse – like we are – like the rest of the herd. And if that isn't enough, blue eyes! Why, our son is a brown and white spotted, blue-eyed horse! This will never do! I'll be laughed right off the Great Plains when the other horses see this spectacle!"

"Calm down, Raven," my mother replied. "I don't know why our son is covered with spots. Perhaps he will become solid when he gets older. But I think he's perfect. Stop making such a fuss. Those eyes! They're the most beautiful shade of blue I have ever seen. What shall we call him?"

"Disaster is appropriate," answered my father.

"I mean, what shall we name our new son? I know. I'll name him Sky Eyes. We'll call him Sky for short. It's perfect!"

My mother reached down to nuzzle me, but Raven turned away. Tears filled my eyes. I heard the rest of the herd consoling him, telling him it would work out, that my color would change with time, that my blue eyes could turn brown. I felt ashamed. I was ugly. My father hated me. Why was I ever born?

Mother saw my tears and tried to comfort me. "I love you so much, Sky. Don't worry. Your father hasn't realized how special your spotted coat and blue eyes will make you someday. You're destined for great things, little one. Never forget that you are loved."

My mother said the things I needed to hear, just when I needed to hear them.

It became obvious that she had more practical things on her mind. She commanded me to stand up. I thought she must be joking! I could not imagine trying to stand up on those wobbly things. But she said I must try, and so I did. I tried, and tried, and tried some more. It seemed that I couldn't quite get my legs to cooperate. I found myself falling down in the most embarrassing ways. Birth seemed easy by comparison! Mother told me I must stand quickly; I would be in danger until I could walk with the herd. Little did I know how right she was!

Suddenly, a loud growling sound came from behind a small bluff nearby. It grew louder and louder until a great grizzly bear appeared. It was Mato (mah-toe)!

My mother squealed in horror. Raven quickly returned to her side, alarmed at the bear's appearance.

"It is old Mato! Run, Star Face," my father warned. "Stay at a safe distance with the others. I will take care of our son."

"I won't leave Sky here," answered my mother.

"Listen to me! I won't risk losing both of you! I will protect him. Now go! Quickly!" Raven watched as Star Face joined the herd.

My father stood before me, shielding me from the great bear. I was frightened beyond belief. Despite my fear, I listened to every word my father and Mato exchanged.

"Why are you here, Mato?" Raven demanded.

"I thought you would be happy to see me, Raven. It has been a long time, and I have traveled far to see your new son," Mato stated.

"How could you know of my son's birth? He was born only a short time ago. Besides, my son is no business of yours," Raven replied sternly.

"On the contrary," boomed the old bear, "your son is very much my business. I see he is a brown and white spotted blue-eyed colt."

"Neither his color nor his birth are your concern! Leave my land now, Mato! You don't belong here," Raven shouted.

"I am beginning to lose my patience, horse! Step aside. Let me do the job I came here to do. I have waited years for this moment. You cannot stop me from completing my mission," thundered Mato.

"I will not permit you near my son!"

With that, Raven reared and lunged toward the bear. In answer, Mato raised his massive paw and delivered a powerful blow to my father's chest. The tremendous force sent Raven flying back behind me, where he collapsed on the ground. He was dazed, but uninjured. As Raven stood, Mato spoke to him, "Give way, Raven. Do not force me to hurt you again. The scars on your neck are a reminder of what I can do when I am angered. Return to the others now. I will finish here shortly. Go!"

Raven recalled the mauling he had received from Mato. As a young stallion, he had wandered too close to the old bear's den. He then realized that an injury to him would jeopardize the welfare of the entire herd. My father was compelled to retreat.

"I do not understand your mission, Mato, but I know that you, too, are a father. Do not harm my son," he pleaded.

Satisfied that my father had gone, Mato turned to me. I struggled to stand, but fear paralyzed every muscle in my body. I closed my eyes, and prepared for the worst. I felt that my short life was going to end as quickly as it had begun!

The great bear moved forward. His immense shadow covered my small body. I could hear my mother's frantic cries. I could feel Mato's breath on my back.

Several moments passed, and nothing happened. Could the bear have left? I decided to take a quick peek. As I opened one eye slowly, Mato's large brown eyes caught mine.

I expected them to be the eyes of a killer. Instead, they were filled with tenderness – soft and gentle. I was no longer afraid. I raised my head from the ground, and Mato caressed my forehead with the same massive paw he had used to strike my father. He began to speak.

"Mother Earth and the entire animal

kingdom have waited a very long time for your arrival. It is hard to believe that you are here before me. I am sorry I frightened your family. It was the only way I could give you my very special gifts in privacy," Mato declared.

He bent down beside me and placed his paws on my back. He touched me once, twice, three times, leaving behind six large bear-paw markings. Once more he spoke to me. "Along with the rest of your spots, you will carry my paw prints upon your back. They will remind you, and the rest of the animal world, that you carry my strength and ferocity, and that you are a great healer. These are my gifts to you, little one. And now, I must go. I have over-stayed my welcome. You shall come to me when you are grown. Remember me, for I will never forget you." The great Mato smiled at me, and I smiled back.

Suddenly, my attention was diverted by the sound of my mother's approach. She had managed to bolt from the corral the herd had created. Her fear was obvious. "Leave my son alone, Mato! Do not hurt him!" she warned.

Mato stared directly into my mother's eyes and said, "Why would I hurt your son, Star Face? It would be like hurting myself, for he and I are one now. But you already suspected that, didn't you?"

My mother said absolutely nothing, but watched cautiously as Mato departed.

At last, I was reunited with my mother. With her warm nose nuzzling mine, I stood for the first time. Together we joined the herd.

We survived our encounter with the great old grizzly, Mato. It was a tale that would be told among the herds on the Great Plains for many years. It was the first of many such tales in which I would be a part.

CHAPTER TWO

My birth day was certainly out of the ordinary, and it gave the family plenty to talk about. My childhood would prove to be no different. The unique coloring of my coat was always a topic of conversation. You see, as I began to grow, I didn't turn into the solid-colored horse everyone hoped I would. My brown spots became more distinct, and my white spots were as bright as freshly fallen snow. The eyes for which I had been named remained blue, and became more brilliant as time passed. If that wasn't enough, the bear-paw marks Mato left grew in size and clarity.

As I said, being the only spotted, blue-eyed colt—touched by a bear at birth—made my childhood difficult, and, at times, very complicated. Looking back, I realize my mother tried to shield me from the herd's gossip. When I became a yearling, she could no longer protect me, as she did when I was a foal.

Not a day went by without insulting remarks from the mares in the herd. When I would pass by, they would turn away and whisper to each other. Of course, it was just loud enough for me to hear.

"I don't know how Star Face does it! It must be difficult raising such a misfit!"

"I heard all those spots made Sky a little slow. You know, in the head. What a pity."

"With those blue eyes, I'm sure he'll be blind before he reaches the age of three!"

By far, the worst talk came from Moonshadow, a silver-gray mare. She was the oldest horse in the herd, and one of the first members of Raven's band. It was said that she was once in love with Raven and wanted to be lead mare. When he chose my mother instead, Moonshadow was devastated. She became a jealous, bitter old mare, remaining with the herd for only one reason: the advancement of her son.

Raven and Moonshadow had a two-year old son, Two Socks. Moonshadow often reminded the herd that her handsome black colt had inherited all the qualities necessary to become the next herd leader. When Raven stepped down, she insisted, Two Socks was the only logical candidate to replace him.

That was, until I was born. Raven and Star Face had agreed that should anything happen to Raven, I would take control of the herd. Because of this, Moonshadow despised me. She did everything in her power to persuade the herd to reject me.

Moonshadow was the instigator behind most of the gossip about me. And to make matters worse, Two Socks tormented me constantly. He teased and mocked me, especially in front of the other yearlings. They would often side with him, calling me names and playing practical jokes. Two Socks made it absolutely impossible for me to get along with my peers, and I often found myself alone.

There was one yearling who paid no attention to Two Socks and his criticism, a filly named White Heart. I remember our first meeting. I thought everything about her was beautiful, especially her rich red chestnut coat and matching mane and tail. The cute, heart-shaped snip on her nose, for which she was named, suited her in more than one way. White Heart was truly pure and gentle of heart.

White Heart was also painfully shy. I was embarrassed about my markings. As a result, we rarely talked. On occasion, our eyes would accidentally meet. I could feel the blood rushing to my face. I am sure I blushed as brightly as a robin's red breast!

In my eyes, White Heart was perfect. I had quite a yearling crush on her, though I knew that a filly of her standing would never associate with a "freak of nature" like me. If we had been seen together, she would surely be as much an outcast as I. I had to be content to watch White Heart from afar, hoping she understood my longings and frustrations.

As I look back, my mother was my best friend. She was the lead mare and a mother figure to all members of the herd. She was required to be teacher, listener, advisor, and sometimes disciplinarian. It was in this role that Mother became my greatest friend and ally. In her role as teacher, she always placed me first among her pupils. As a listener, she heard with sympathy all my fears and concerns. Her advice was both wise and fair.

Often at night, just as we youngsters were preparing for sleep, Star Face would tell us tales of Mother Earth and her creatures. She spoke often of the Great Plains, our home. I learned that the Plains were the daughters of Mother Earth. They were vast, beautiful lands of sun, wind, and grass. Thousands of miles stretched between the arms of the Plains. Crystal clear streams crossed their bodies. Lush, sweet grasslands abounded. For their robes, the Plains wore the sky. All the animals, whether furred, feathered, or scaled, owed their well-being to the Great Plains. They could fill our hearts with joy.

But the Great Plains were fickle, too, cautioned Mother. As beautiful and generous as they were, they could also be temperamental and dangerous. Summers often brought violent thunderstorms and tornadoes. Winters brought fierce blizzards and huge snowfalls. Dramatic changes in climate, where temperatures dropped as much as 50 degrees, were the rule. Months of drought could be followed by sudden blasts of blinding rain or icy sheets of hail. At other times, searing, gale-strength winds could rage out of the south to wither the grass, and threaten all the creatures of the plains.

My mother reminded us that the animals living on the plains were strong enough to survive such weather tantrums. No matter what we had to endure, the Great Plains were well loved by all its inhabitants.

More grim lessons were saved for the light of day. Star Face often spoke about Mother Earth's cardinal rule: survival of the fittest. There were the hunters and the hunted, she explained. Wild horses, unfortunately, fell into the latter category. We had to be always on guard, watchful of coyotes, big cats such as mountain lions, and worst of all, packs of hungry wolves. They preyed upon the herds, and often killed the young.

History lessons concerned our arrival on the Great Plains. Back then, the herds that thrived on the plains were actually relative newcomers. Mother told us how our ancestors were brought to North America from distant lands by human beings. Some horses chose to continue their work with humans. Others broke that bond and struck out on their own. These adventure-seekers finally made their way to the "Land of Never Ending Prairie," the Great Plains.

At first, our ancestors had a lot to learn about the Great Plains. They might have perished if it were not for the oldest and wisest inhabitants – the buffalo. For centuries, the buffalo had flourished on the plains. They accepted horses into their homeland, guided, and protected us. As a result, the wild horse herds grew and expanded.

There were many herds scattered across the plains. Our family herd was the largest. When I was a yearling, there were 30 mares, some with foals. Eleven juvenile colts lived under the protection of the herd as well, bringing our family to sixty-one members.

I enjoyed my mother's lessons and stories, but I most treasured our time alone together. She showered me with love. She told me all about my father, Raven. He was legendary; known throughout the region for his strength, courage, and intelligence. He was a powerful equine figure, fairly ruling the herd, yet often displaying a gentle and understanding heart. He remained unchallenged, for there was no horse who did not admire and respect him.

Mere mention of his name conjures up my favorite image of my father. As a youngster, I loved to watch him on top of his favorite lookout hill. He was so intent with the job at hand – guarding the herd. Motionless, he remained on that hill for hours, never once removing his eyes from his grazing family below. It was as if he had turned into a magnificent stone statue. His long mane and tail blew gracefully in the gentle prairie breeze. Sunlight danced in shades of blue across his ebony coat. So noble and regal was this figure of a horse. So free and untamed was his spirit! This was the vision of a true leader, and I was proud to be his son.

Of course, Mother reminded me, Raven's free spirit had been tamed – by her. She was as beautiful and sweet as Raven was great. My father could not resist the gold of her mane and tail and the sheen of her chestnut coat. The perfect white star between her soft brown eyes was matched by a kind and loving disposition. I always felt safe and secure when I was with her.

I had another special friend. I often wished that it had been my father. Unfortunately, he remained distant during most of my childhood. His position as head of the herd occupied him constantly. No. My wonderful friend was the magical mountain range that lay to the north of the plains, the Black Hills.

It was my mother's lessons that had first introduced me to the Black Hills. She told romantic tales about this oldest of mountains. It was "the heart of everything that is." She described it as possessing dark, pine-forested bluffs which rose out of an ocean of grass like a mysterious island. The beauty of the Black Hills was only surpassed by its supernatural powers. It was the home of the animals of the spirit world. Mere mortal animals were forbidden to trespass on the magical mountain range.

From the moment I first heard my mother's story, I was left with a powerful attraction and tremendous curiosity. I spent endless hours just watching and memorizing every feature of my stony companion's silhouette. Soon after, I realized that a strong relationship had developed between us. The Black Hills had become my secret friend.

Each and every day I looked forward to the quiet time we would spend together. Every morning, just before sunrise, I raced to the top of my father's lookout hill and gazed off into the distance.

At dawn, my friend patiently waited for the sun to warm and awaken him from his peaceful slumber. As the sun moved across the sky, the face of the Black Hills became a spectacular display. Every color of the rainbow was reflected from his stony surface into the clouds above. As the rest of the herd slept, I was thrilled by this grand performance. I was sure that it was designed for my eyes only.

The Black Hills and I shared much more than these magical daybreaks. Whenever I felt really alone, sad or blue, I just looked at my friend. Knowing that he would always be there filled me with comfort and security, banishing my loneliness.

Sometimes the Black Hills spoke to me, telling his ancient tales. His descriptions of the lands on his far side were equally fascinating. He often expressed a desire for me to pay him a visit, but as much as

I longed to see his impressive face, I did not dare anger the Great Plains. Attempting a visit might risk the lives of everyone in the herd.

I was grateful for my friendship with the Black Hills, but I also hoped that this secret friendship would remain unnoticed by the other members of the family herd. Unfortunately, that was not meant to be. They named me "Mountain Gazer" behind my back, adding that to their long list of insults. I was taunted by Two Socks and then by the rest of the yearlings. I was the "horse of a different color" who spoke to mountains. But this didn't trouble me. My special relationship with the great mountain range was too important. It could not be damaged by ignorant horses who lacked understanding.

Yes, my childhood was difficult at times. It wasn't easy being a horse of a different color on the Great Plains. With my mother's words of encouragement and the inspiration of the Black Hills, I coped.

For the first year of my life I was relatively content – until one day in late summer. That day changed my life forever.

CHAPTER THREE

I had just completed my morning visit with the Black Hills. The rest of the herd was finishing their breakfast. The yearlings frolicked in the tall prairie grass nearby, and I heard them planning a game of hide-and-seek.

As I came down from my father's hill, one of the yearlings called out to me, "Sky, quick, go and hide. Grey Cloud is 'It' and he has already started counting to ten!"

I remember that I was shocked. Were they having a change of heart? As I raced to find a good hiding place, my heart pounded with excitement. They were finally going to accept me, with my blue eyes, spots and all. I was so happy to be included in their game.

I found a great hiding place behind some large boulders that were partially concealed by patches of scrub brush. I nestled down between the rocks and waited for Grey Cloud to find me.

I waited and waited. There was no sign of him. I thought to myself that I must have chosen the best hiding place in the world! I continued to wait. Finally, I realized that Grey Cloud was not going to find me. He wasn't even looking. Hours had passed. It had all been a joke. Tears ran down my face.

I hated the other yearlings! I hated the herd! I hated my life on the Great Plains! Why was I so different from the others? My mother was all wrong. I was not special. I felt the only thing I was capable of achieving was hiding behind boulders.

Over my sobs, I heard the sound of another horse approaching. As I rose, shaking the tears from my eyes, I looked up to see White Heart standing before me. I was so startled that I stumbled over my own hooves and went sprawling to the ground. She stepped forward to help me.

"Are you all right, Sky? Are you hurt? That was a terrible trick the others played on you! I don't blame you for being upset.

If I were a colt and a few hands taller, I'd show those bullies a thing or two!" she said heatedly.

White Heart helped me to my feet, and to my embarrassment, began cleaning my dusty coat with her perfect tail.

"Oh, uh, you don't have to do that, White Heart. Uh ... I'll be okay," I stammered.

In fact, I was so embarrassed that I could barely speak. I kept stumbling over my words. Yet, I was thrilled to be standing next to this perfect filly. Thankfully, she took no notice and went right on talking. "I'm glad you're not hurt. You really did find a great hiding place. It took me almost an hour to find you after I realized what the others had done. Your spots provide excellent camouflage. You blend right in with the boulders. You see, your spots are good for something! If you had kept quiet, I would have gone right past you. I'll bet no horse alive could find you in a game of hide-and-seek."

Just like my mother, White Heart said exactly what I needed to hear, at the moment I needed to hear it. I loved her for that. Timidly, we touched noses. Then we headed back to the herd.

As we neared the other horses, we heard the cries from one of the older colts, "Herd approaching! Herd coming in fast from the south! Looks like seven or eight with a big dun in the lead."

White Heart and I reached the herd just as they closed ranks. Raven stood in front. I stood behind him, next to my mother, as befit my station.

It was not the first time we had visiting herds in our territory. Many herds had traveled great distances to see the brown and white spotted blue-eyed son of Raven. At first, I hated the visitors and their rude comments and questions. Eventually, I grew accustomed to them and rarely showed outright disgust at their visits. When I did, my mother would encourage me to be polite with a swift nip to my neck. Fortunately, my parents had become skillful at handling these uncomfortable visits, and my neck was most often spared.

On that day, watching and waiting was difficult. I tried to remain focused, but my thoughts kept drifting back to my encounter with White Heart. Despite the humiliation I had suffered at the hooves of the yearlings, I had a wonderful day because of White Heart's kindness. I was convinced that additional insults and rude stares from visitors would have no effect on me. But I was not prepared for the event that followed.

Several minutes passed before the weary visitors came into view. There were eight mares led by a large dun stallion. As they approached my father, they appeared tired, beaten, and almost fragile. Coats were dull, dusty, and sun-bleached. Manes and tails were worn thin and tangled from sand-filled windstorms. Their ears and noses were burnt and peeling from exposure to the sun. Most shocking of all, protruding ribs spoke of the scarcity of food and water on their journey. I could see the concern in my father's eyes as he stepped forward to address the dun.

"Welcome to my territory. I don't believe we've met. I am Raven, and these grasslands are mine. You must be weary after your long journey. I am a bit worried about the condition of your mares," Raven said.

"The condition of my mares is not your business, Raven. And no, we have not met before. I am Sandstorm, the new leader of the southern herd. This spring I defeated Redmane, and took command of his herd. He was killed soon after by a pack of wolves. We have come here to see your famous son, Sky. I had to see this spotted freak of the northern plains for myself," the dun concluded.

"I will not tolerate insults from you, or any member of your herd, while you stand on my land. Keep your remarks to yourself," warned Raven. "As for Redmane, I was not aware of his death," he continued. "He was a good friend. Had I known, I would have gone to pay my respects. But what happened to the rest of his herd? The last I saw Redmane, his herd boasted twenty to thirty members. What has become of them?"

These questions seemed to annoy Sandstorm. "The great drought killed most of those weak, whining excuses for mares. These eight are all that remain of Redmane's herd. Now, they are devoted to me," Sandstorm asserted.

"Are you trying to divert my attention from your son, Raven?" the dun asked, turning to a less painful subject. "Is that him standing behind you? Have him step forward so we may all see him. Or do you find such viewing too embarrassing?" Sandstorm cajoled.

I did not have time to step forward. At that very moment, Moonshadow and Two Socks broke rank from the bulk of the herd and positioned themselves in front of Sandstorm.

"I, at least, am pleased to meet you Sandstorm," Moonshadow interrupted smoothly. "My name is Moonshadow, and this is my handsome son, Two Socks. Unfortunately, his future as the next herd-leader has been taken by the spotted freak you have come to see. Look for yourself. That thing could never rule. His herd would be too busy laughing at his spots and weak blue eyes. His commands would never be followed. Now, take a look at my handsome boy. He is strong, sound, and smart!" she bragged. "Turn around, Two Socks," Moonshadow commanded her son. "Let this noble stallion get a good look at a future leader."

Two Socks did as his mother directed, prancing around in front of Sandstorm and his mares. The mares seemed to be impressed, but Sandstorm grew angry. Suddenly, he reared up and lunged forward, striking Two Socks hard across his face. The youngster cried out in pain and fell to his knees.

"Let that nasty bruise serve as a warning, proud one! Never consider challenging me. I am Sandstorm, the southern king. As for you Moonshadow," the dun said, turning disdainfully to the mare, "how Raven can permit you to speak so boldly here, in front of strangers, is beyond my understanding. Does he have no control over his mares?"

"Enough!" seethed Raven. He walked slowly toward Sandstorm, his neck arching in rage. "It sounds as though you wish to challenge my leadership, Sandstorm. Leave now or prepare to defend yourself."

I wondered if it was all really happening. Many questions began to race through my mind. Who would have the audacity to challenge Raven? His prowess was legendary. Would Raven be strong enough to defend the herd, or would he be driven away forever? Would he survive the challenge?

My family backed away from the two stallions. I saw Sandstorm's mares retreat, as well.

"What is your answer, horse?"

demanded Raven. "Will you fight, or will you flee?"

Sandstorm stood his ground. "I will fight," he trumpeted. I screamed, "No, Father, no!" My frantic cry went unnoticed.

The clash of hooves announced the beginning of the battle. Nothing could stop it. My mother tried to block my view. She told me not to watch, that I was too young. Frightened, I buried my face in her long golden mane. But even my fear did not prevent me from watching the fight. Along with the rest of the family, I gazed on in horror.

The pounding of hooves and angry cries echoed over the prairie. The stallions reared skyward. Their muscles were straining, as their legs pawed the air in fury. With ears pinned back and teeth bared, Raven lunged for his opponents' withers. In anticipation, Sandstorm turned sharply and kicked out. His razor-sharp back hooves left a serious gash on my father's foreleg. Raven jerked back, as blood streamed down his leg. The dun seized the opportunity to press the attack and proceeded to bite and nip the injured leg. Raven dropped to his knees, to prevent the challenger from causing additional damage. Sandstorm, a wily fighter, mimicked my father's movement.

Through the churning dust, the stallions continued their vicious assault on exposed legs. They both realized that sufficient injury to an opponent's legs would lead to a quick victory.

Raven managed to inflict an exacting bite to the dun's knee. Sandstorm briefly lowered his eyes to inspect his wound and foolishly dropped his guard. It was the moment for which my father had been waiting. In seconds, he jumped back up on all four legs. Before Sandstorm could rise and gain his balance, Raven wheeled and delivered a powerful kick to the dun's hindquarters. Sandstorm squealed in agony and fell hard on his side.

A tense silence enveloped the herd, as Raven stood over Sandstorm's crumpled body. We waited for our leader to destroy his enemy, but the rage began to leave his eyes. Then, he did something that surprised all of us. He sighed deeply, shook his head, and slowly walked away. The fight was over as quickly as it had begun.

Sandstorm's mares raced past Raven to

assist their leader. My father, however, was not completely finished with him. "Sandstorm, I cannot believe that you defeated Redmane fairly. I think you ended his life through some foul play. Redmane was a great wolf-fighter. I know. In our early years together we could chase off any wolf pack on the Great Plains. As for the rest of Redmane's herd, your poor leadership was undoubtedly the cause of their deaths. As a leader, I despise you for that. Your mares are in need of rest, plenty of sweet grass, and water. A short distance from here is one of my favorite grazing lands. Nearby is a stream. Take your mares there and stay until you have regained your strength. When you are well enough to travel, leave my land. Take Moonshadow and Two Socks. They will remain with you until they learn respect and tolerance for all members of my herd. Remember Sandstorm, you will never again set hoof in my domain, until you learn what it is to be a true leader."

Having said this, Raven's eyes searched for Star Face. Knowingly, she cantered to my father's side. Without speaking, she looked intently into his weary eyes. Her sigh of relief was answered by a reassuring wink.

I saw my father in a new light. He limped past me, covered with sweat, blood, and dust, his mane was tangled and matted. I stared, in complete awe of him. I realized that on that very day, at that precise moment, my father had become my hero.

With that realization came another, a more painful one. I was the cause of all my hero's problems. Ever since my birth there was constant unrest in the herd. They no longer worked together or looked after one another. They were no longer a tightly knit herd.

I remember thinking that the unceasing criticism and concerns about my appearance were not likely to end. I burdened my father with the necessity of having to both reprimand and reassure the herd on a daily basis. His choice to make me the next leader was unpopular with many. Raven could not convince them that his blue-eyed spotted son would ever possess the knowledge, strength and courage to rule effectively. They did not believe that I could maintain my father's territory. They feared challengers, like Sandstorm, who would certainly come to fight the 'horse of a different color'. Our herd was disintegrating right before my eyes. My parents were unable to stop it. I loved my family deeply, and I cared greatly for White Heart. I refused to see their world destroyed because of me. It was easy to convince myself that they would be better off with me gone.

I realized that I could never be like Raven. Living up to his reputation and expectations was impossible. I feared that I would only shatter my hero's dreams and cause additional family strife. The time had come for me to strike out on my own, to pay that long overdue visit to the Black Hills. I decided to leave and never return. I chose to defy the Great Plains and live the rest of my life on the magical mountain range.

CHAPTER FOUR

The Great Plains ended that fateful day with a spectacular sunset. The moon rose as a great glowing ball, and seemed more brilliant than ever. It illuminated the prairie below, creating an atmosphere of magic. The stars, too, seemed to have grown in size and number as they danced around their heavenly companion. Even the Black Hills was awake that evening, his serene face aglow with celestial light. It was as if they all knew my secret and beckoned me onward.

The day's events had taken their toll on the herd. The family slept in exhaustion – even Raven. For the only time in my memory, he was not on guard duty. My mother had insisted that he rest and nurse his wounds. The challenge he had faced had been stressful. In his place one of the older colts guarded the herd. I felt my luck was turning; it would be easier to slip past an adolescent than my father.

I pretended to be asleep. Finally, after what felt like an eternity, the time came to make my move. I rose quietly. With great stealth, I eased around the sleeping horses. Clouds swept briefly across the moon, aiding my escape. It was easy to get by the colt on watch.

Still moving slowly, I reached the northern perimeter of the herd. I was about to embark on a new stage in my life. I stopped to smell the cool, crisp night air and stared at the vast, slumbering prairie. My adventure was just beginning. Somewhere, out there was my new life.

Just as I prepared to turn my back on the herd, I was startled to feel something soft and warm on my right flank. Alarmed, I jumped straight up off the ground. I turned and found myself looking, once again, into the eyes of White Heart. At that moment, they were filled with concern and confusion.

"White Heart," I whispered, "you nearly scared the spots right off my back! What are you doing here?"

"I missed you in your usual sleeping spot," she said softly. "And I was worried. I came to find you."

"Shhh. Keep your voice down. I don't want to wake the others," I urged. "But how did you know where I sleep? I didn't think you noticed."

"Oh," White Heart whispered in turn, "there are a great many things about you I've noticed, Sky. But what are you doing here?"

"If you must know, I'm running away. I've caused too many problems for the herd. You'll be better off without me," I retorted, my voice deepening.

"Sky, what about your mother and father? They'll miss you terribly. And so will I. Where can you possibly go?" she asked.

"I'm going to miss you and my parents, but I've made up my mind. There is nothing you can do to stop me. I am going to visit a friend," I said firmly.

White Heart would not be discouraged. "Please," she implored, "take me with you."

"No. It's dangerous and I must do this alone. Stay with the herd. Don't worry.

Some day I will return. Farewell, White Heart."

I turned away from White Heart, embarrassed at the tears that were filling my eyes. As I walked out into the night, I heard her whisper softly, "Goodbye, Sky. Take care of yourself. I will miss you. I ... I love you."

Though her words touched me deeply, I refused to look back. I truly believed the grass had to be greener on the other side of the Black Hills. I was the brown and white spotted blue-eyed colt who was determined to find out.

When I was sure that I would not awaken the herd, I galloped as fast as my legs would carry me, for miles and miles, ever onward, through a darkening sea of grass. I had to keep moving. I had to distance myself from the herd.

I kept my thoughts from drifting to images of wolves and other fearful dangers by focusing on the noble face of the Black Hills. Over and over, I repeated the same words, "I belong with you, my friend. I am coming as fast as I can. Soon we will be together, for I belong with you."

After a time, I could see out of the corner of my eye, a great shadow moving toward me. Frightened, I veered away to avoid a collision. I stopped in my tracks and felt the hair on the back of my neck standing straight up. Loud moaning sounds came from the area in which I had first seen the threatening shadow.

"Mmmmmm, mmmmm. Who goes there? Step out into the moonlight where I can see you," thrummed a deep voice.

Fearful at first, I was relieved to see Tanka (tahn-kah), the aged buffalo cow, emerge from the gloom. I moved forward to greet her.

"I am sorry to disturb you, Tanka. It is Sky, son of Raven," I said respectfully.

"So, it is the Painted Prince," she responded. "What brings you out into the plains in the middle of the night? It is quite dangerous for a horse to be traveling alone, you know. Could you be running away from home, little one?"

"How could you know that, Tanka?" I asked suspiciously.

"Oh, I have my sources. Now, where are you headed on this magical night?" she inquired.

"Well, you're going to think I'm

crazy ... but I am going to visit my friend, the Black Hills. You see, Tanka, the mountains talk to me, though you may laugh to hear it said," I blurted out.

"I will not laugh, Sky, nor do I think you foolish. The Black Hills talk to me as well. You forget that I am the younger sister of the Great Plains. The mountains often speak to me. You must be very special." Tanka declared. "The Great Plains do not allow just any animal to hear their favorite mountains. You, little horse, are very special, indeed. Now, tell me, why do you feel compelled to run away from your family herd?"

Though I was not eager to share my feelings with Tanka, I respected her wisdom and position on the plains. My story began to pour out. "Oh, Tanka! I am causing so many problems for my parents and the herd. It is not just the mockery my peers make of me. It is the feeling of isolation and rejection that hurts so deeply. They don't understand me. They don't try. My life is miserable!" I explained, clearly distressed.

"Now, now, little prince. You have to understand that horses are, by buffalo standards, newcomers to the plains. They haven't yet discovered what my family learned long ago – tolerance for things that are different.

"Different can be wonderful and special, Sky. Your spots and eyes make you unique. You are blessed. The entire animal kingdom respects your difference. We have waited many hundred of years for your arrival on Mother Earth. Alas, your own species still has much to learn," she sighed.

"Do not take their criticisms to heart. Believe in yourself. Some day, you will accomplish great things. You are destined to become a king among horses. The entire animal world will bow before you," Tanka proclaimed.

"I ... I don't understand what you are saying, Tanka," I stammered. My weariness, the stress of the day, the surprise of coming upon Tanka, all those things combined to cloud my judgement. I could not comprehend the story that Tanka was trying to tell me.

As I yawned, she stated, "I believe it is well past the usual hour for your bed, my Painted Prince. Now is not the time for explanations. You need rest before you continue your journey. Come join my herd tonight. You are welcome to sleep near the calves. You will be completely out of harms way," she hummed sympathetically.

The old cow led me to the center of the herd, where the young calves slept peacefully. I noticed one that was very different from the rest. She was pure white! I stared in spite of myself.

"You see the newest member of my herd, Sky. Her name is Waniyetu (Wah-nee-yea-do). Like you, she is different. And, like you, she is a very special gift from Mother Earth. Our pride is boundless. We are truly blessed," boasted Tanka.

It was easy to understand Tanka's pride. The calf was a true beauty.

"She is so lovely, Tanka! Pure and perfect, like the freshly fallen snow of winter," I exclaimed. "She must be very special!"

"Yes, Sky, she is. But so are you," Tanka replied. "You have already learned what no other in your herd has. You have learned tolerance and appreciation for the beauty and qualities of being different.

"Go to sleep now, little one. Sleep and dream the dreams of the kings of the plains."

I gratefully obeyed Tanka's order and laid down beside the tiny white buffalo calf. Waniyetu rolled over and raised her head to look at me. Smiling sleepily, she snuggled against my spotted coat. Her trust made me feel honored.

For a moment, before surrendering to sleep, I thought of my family. I longed for the day they would be able to see past my brown and white spotted coat, as Tanka and Waniyetu had. I wanted them to look into my blue eyes and see – not a freak – but an ordinary horse. No prince, no king, just me – Sky, the son of Raven and Star Face.

I was just too tired to make sense of Tanka's words. I hoped the morning would bring understanding. At last, I drifted off to sleep.

Chapter Five

Too soon, daybreak arrived. I awoke to the unfamiliar grunts, moans, and bellows of the buffalo herd. Yawning, I rose to my feet and shook myself awake.

Tanka approached and invited me to join her for breakfast. I grazed alongside her family herd for nearly an hour before preparing to leave.

I thanked the old cow for her hospitality and kind words, and headed north. In the distance, waiting patiently, was my old friend the Black Hills. I realized it would be only a few days before I reached my destination. Tanka, little Waniyetu, and the rest of the herd stood in formation and watched as I resumed my journey.

The Great Plains provided a beautiful morning for my continuing adventure. For many miles, I galloped effortlessly across her until the rising heat of the day forced me to stop for a short rest.

I found a winding stream and thought it would be a perfect place for a drink. The stream was crystal clear and inviting, but my mother's lessons made me cautious. I didn't want to disturb Unktehi (unk-tay-hee), the spirit of the water. The giant monster, whose body nourished the animal world, was a powerful but often dangerous creature. He could rise up without warning, engulf his victims, and drown them. Some animals were allowed to drink and swim across his watery body, while others were destroyed in violent rapids and whirlpools. There was no predicting what the Unktehi would do.

Mother had taught me great respect for the water. It was only safe to drink if the water monster was asleep. On that day, I was fortunate, Unktehi was sleeping soundly. I approached the water's edge carefully and took a long, deep drink.

As I backed away from the stream feeling refreshed, my right rear hoof hit something hard. The object made a loud thud, then cried out furiously.

"You stupid animal! You stepped right on me and almost crushed my beautiful home! Come down here where I can see the clumsy oaf that nearly destroyed my perfect shell."

Curious, I lowered my head. Staring at me was the face of an ancient turtle. "I'm terribly sorry, Mr. Turtle," I apologized. "I didn't mean any harm."

But the turtle was not pleased. He snapped at me. I jumped back in the nick of time.

"It's Kela (kay-lah) to you! My name is Kela. Don't you have any respect for your elders?" he asked indignantly. "Don't you ever look where you're going, you young whipper-snapper? You could have caused me serious injury!" He paused, squinting up at me. "What are you anyway?"

"I'm a horse, Kela. My name is Sky. I just stopped by for a drink, and ... "

"A horse, you say!" he interrupted. "What are you doing out here without your herd? Don't you know that you are only safe when you are with your herd? You must be awfully dumb to be traveling alone. Now, lower your head so I can get a better look at you, foolish horse," Kela demanded.

I lowered my head once again. The old turtle scrunched up his eyes and examined my face. I suspected his eyesight might be growing dim due to his advanced age, so I gave him plenty of time.

"Well, I see a big nose. But what is this? Blue eyes? Do you have blue eyes, son? What is this? I see spots before my eyes! You have spots all over the place! Why, you are a brown and white spotted blue-eyed horse. Oh my! Oh dear! You are the one! I don't believe my eyes! You are the Painted Prince! How dare you show up now! You made me wait two hundred years, and now you show up unannounced! Now, when I'm so old I can't remember what I am supposed to do when you finally arrive.

"What was that thing Mother Earth told me – long, long ago? What do I have to do? Oh, what was it? Hmmm, I think it had something to do with a gift. You were supposed to bring me a gift. No, that's not right. Uh, I was to see how gifted you are at some thing. No, hmmm, that's not right, either. Oh, now what was it? You see how difficult it can be when you have lived a long, long life?"

I didn't understand what he was talking about, but I was thinking about his unpleasant attitude. Old age had certainly made him grumpy and extremely rude. Still, I respected the turtle. His shell was covered with years of mud and moss. In his wrinkled old face I could see knowledge and wisdom. It was unfortunate that his memory was failing. I could have learned much from a turtle who had seen two hundred years of life on the Great Plains.

Suddenly, Kela cried, "That's it! I remember now! I was to give you gifts. Special gifts; the kind that only I can give. Well, are ya ready, horse? Is the Painted Prince ready to receive my gifts?"

"I will be deeply honored to accept your gifts," I responded, as my mother had taught me.

"Oh, shut your mouth and accept the gifts already! I give to you, the Great Plains' first and only spotted blue-eyed horse, my gifts of good health and long life.

"Well? Well? Aren't you gonna thank me, you ungrateful, equine snip?" Kela demanded.

I wanted to be gracious, but in truth I could neither see nor smell Kela's gifts.

"Why, of course. Thank you, Kela," I managed to stammer. "I ... I don't understand your gifts. But, of course, I am grateful just the same."

"My gifts of good health and immortality cannot be seen, or smelled, or tasted, horse!" Kela said, exasperated. "It becomes a part of you. Here, deep inside. So just say thank you. Now, go away! All this excitement has made me very tired all of a sudden. You can't expect me to be pleasant when you come here without an appointment. I'm so very, very sleepy," he murmured, drowsily, and fell asleep right before me.

My heart went out to old Kela. He had gotten himself into quite a dither when he saw me. I realized it was his aging mind and body that had really frustrated him, rather than my surprise appearance. I guess he earned the right to be a bit difficult and grumpy.

As I watched the turtle sleep, I recognized my own need for rest. I, too, was exhausted. My journey and the encounter with Kela had tired me out. Close by, I noticed an area of tall grass shaded by the trunk of a dying tree. It was an ideal place for a peaceful afternoon nap. I could see no reason to continue, when such a bed beckoned. I did not realize that napping was the last thing I would do in the sweet grass.

The grass felt wonderfully cool against my coat. I suddenly had the uncontrollable urge to roll. Back and forth I went, with my legs flying in every direction. No itch went unattended. I yawned and stretched out for what I thought would be a peaceful nap. Just as I began to fall asleep, I heard a soft fluttering sound around my ears. First one ear, then the other. Next, I felt the fluttering of wings, tiny little wings. I shook my head. Thankfully, the noise stopped.

A moment later, the fluttering began again, but it was around my nose. All at once, something made a landing between my nostrils. I sneezed! The pest was crawling up my face towards my eyes, completely undeterred by my efforts. What a nuisance! That insect needed to learn some manners, I thought. I opened my eyes with the intention of disciplining the flying annoyance. Peering down at me, was a large, yellow butterfly.

"Ah, so you're awake. Allow me to

introduce myself. My name is Kimi Mila
(kee-mee mee-lah). I have come to pay my
respects to the Painted Prince." Kimi
Mila's voice was surprisingly soft and
breathy, and I found myself pricking my
ears forward to hear him.

"Forgive me, Kimi Mila, if I seemed
impolite. I was trying to take a nap,"
I explained, with a smile on my face.

"Oh, there's plenty of time for that. My
mission is very urgent. I have come to give
you my own very special gift," he said, as
his wings pumped in ceremony.

"I'm very flattered, little friend. But
what could a butterfly possibly give to a
horse?" I inquired.

"Oh, you must not discount my size.
You know the old saying – good things
come from small packages – or something
like that," he muttered. "Well, anyway, I
have something very precious, indeed, to
give to you, Sunka Wakan. Oops! Uh, I
mean, to you great Painted Prince ... uh,"
the butterfly hesitated in confusion.

Obviously something he said caused
Kimi Mila discomfort. What was it? I had
little time to ponder before he began again.

"It is the power to detect and elude
danger that I give you," he continued.

"Now, it's time for me to be off. Bye!" he concluded in haste, and quickly flew away.

"Wait, Kimi Mila! I don't understand this gift you have given me. And why did you call me that name?" I said, arising from my bed of grass. But I could not stop him. The butterfly had taken flight and disappeared from view.

Back then, none of it made sense to me. At birth I was given a gift from old Mato, the grizzly. I could see his gift on my back. But the gifts from Kela and Kimi Mila were beyond me. I could not see or touch them. I didn't feel any differently having received them. I knew I should feel gratitude – these animals believed strongly in their gifts. I supposed I would have to simply accept them and be thankful for the spirit in which they were given.

Most of all, I was disturbed by the name Kimi Mila used – Sunka Wakan. I had heard that name before. When I was very young, my mother would sing a lullaby. Sunka Wakan was in that lullaby. But who was he, and why had Kimi Mila mentioned his name? It was all very confusing, especially for a tired, brown and white spotted blue-eyed colt.

Again, I prepared to rest, trying at the same time to remember my mother's lullaby. The memory of her soothing voice gave me great comfort as I slowly drifted off into a sound sleep.

I dreamed of my family herd. I dreamed of returning home. The entire herd was cheering. I was their hero. My father was telling me how proud he was of my great act of bravery. White Heart was standing by his side. She was about to speak ... I was suddenly awakened by something very wet and cold. My eyes flew open and my neck jerked upright. As I tried to focus my eyes, a spray of water hit me directly in my face. I shook my head and rose to my feet.

It sounded like something was splashing and giggling in the stream a few feet away. Searching for the source of the disturbance, I trotted to the rocky edge of the stream. Nothing happened. As I turned away, a huge geyser of water flew out of the stream and soaked my coat – spots and all. Laughter filled the air.

Drenched and bewildered, it was hard for me to share in the laughter. I spun around and angrily addressed the stream. "I don't think this is funny. Who is out there? Who is splashing me?" I asserted, trying to sound in command of the situation.

"Hee, tee-hee-hee! It's only me," a voice gurgled, trying to suppress another bubble of laughter. It belonged to a portly, auburn-furred creature who swam swiftly to the shoreline. He climbed onto the rocks and waddled over to me, dragging a huge, paddle-like tail behind him. An air of humor followed in his wake. It was a mischievous beaver.

"Ta-hee, hee, hee," he continued to giggle. "Oh, I am so sorry. I could not resist. You were sleeping so soundly, I just could not control the urge to splash you. Besides, you looked so funny when I splashed you, your face all full of water! Ta-ha!" he said, hugging his sides with the joy of his prank.

His laughter was infectious, and soon I joined in. "Well," I responded in kind, "It wasn't very polite. But, ha-ha, I guess I would have done the same thing if I had been in your position. Ha, ha. I must have looked pretty silly! Hey beaver, what is your name? I am ... "

"Sky," he said before I could finish the introduction. "I know. I am known as

Canyataniwan (Chahn-yah-tah-nee-wahn). But everybody calls me Capa (chah-pah) for short."

"Pleased to meet you, Capa. I was resting from my morning journey. I'm going to visit my old friend ... "

"The Black Hills. I know," he again interrupted. I wondered if he knew everything.

"You know, it's not much farther. You could make it by nightfall, if you leave now," Capa concluded.

"How is it that you know so much about me, Capa?" I asked.

"Wambli (wahm-blee) told me you were coming. I would have arrived sooner, but I had to repair my home. I had difficulty finding the exact log that would correct the problem," Capa responded with an air of distraction.

"Who is Wambli? I don't believe I've met an animal by that name," I queried.

"Oh, you will, and soon," interjected Capa. "Right now, let's take care of the important business at hand. I have to give you my special gift. This is way cool! Are you ready, little horse?" Capa stood to his full height, looking puffed up and a little vain, no indication of the merry prankster left in him. "I, Canyataniwan, better known as Capa, the swiftest and strongest water-animal on Mother Earth," he added, "wish to bestow upon you, my gift. You, Painted Prince, will now and forever be a powerful swimmer with no fear of the water. So be it!" His tail slapped the mud with a powerful smack, finalizing his declaration.

"Well, gee, that wasn't so hard, was it?" he said, resuming in his formerly whimsical tone.

Throughout this ceremony, I stood watching the beaver shift back and forth from comedian to patron, and back again.

"Thank you, Capa," I said, my smile lingering. "Your gift is unique. I just need to ask you one question. How do you swim in Unktehi's body without the monster harming you?"

"It's nothing," said Capa, dismissively. "I am too strong a swimmer to be drowned. We sorta made a pack, years ago. Unktehi allows me to build my home of sticks and logs across his body. In turn, my home acts as a dam for the many fish that live in Unktehi. I, and many other animals, rely on fish for food. My dam provides an excellent area to catch them. The water monster would have a terrible bellyache if we didn't remove some of the fish from his body. So we all benefit. It's really simple. Now, Painted Prince, you should consider my suggestion. You can make it across the plains before nightfall, if you leave now."

"You are right, my friend. I still have plenty of daylight. I am really quite anxious to see the Black Hills. I enjoyed meeting you, Capa. Take care of yourself."

"Oh, you don't have to worry about me. Remember, I'm Capa, the greatest swimmer who ever lived!" And with that, the beaver turned and dove into the shimmering stream.

I realized that by evening, my journey would be over and I would be in my new home, the home where I belonged. I was giddy with anticipation. I reared up in joy. I bucked, and kicked, and whinnied loudly to the Great Plains.

I turned to the north and took off at a full gallop. My friend's smiling face showed me the way.

CHAPTER SIX

Hours passed like minutes. The miles flew by in an endless stream. My hoofbeats echoed like thunder across the vast stretch of plains, announcing my passing to all its residents. The muscles of my shoulders and legs burned and twitched with effort. On and on I galloped, wind pounding my face. Behind me, thick clouds of dust billowed out, like rising smoke from a summer grass fire.

I passed bustling colonies of prairie dogs, their alert sentinels rising up on hindquarters, barking and cheering my passage. From above, a flock of crows cawed out their encouragement. I whinnied to acknowledge their presence, without missing a single hoofbeat.

The landscape began to change dramatically. The flat prairie, with its tall swaying grass, began to rise giving way to gently rolling hills covered by wildflowers. Lofty spires of rock thrust skyward. Sagebrush and prickly pears hugged their rocky bases.

Finally, a grand forest of quaking aspen, juniper, and ponderosa pine took shape. I stopped dead in my tracks and stood with my eyes and mouth wide open, staring at Mother Earth's wondrous creation.

I was completely surrounded by acres of dense forest interspersed with giant rock formations. From my elevated vantage point, I saw high lakes, spectacular canyons with waterfalls, caves, and beautiful streams.

I wondered, could this be the place where horses go when they die? I reached down and nipped my front leg to make sure I was among the living. I was, and I was home. I had finally reached the sacred lands of the Black Hills.

A rustling sound, followed by movement, announced a presence before me. I held my breath. Slowly, and with stately grace, a handsome elk stepped out from behind a cluster of small pines.

"Do not be frightened, little Prince. Allow me to introduce myself. My name is Wapiti (wah-pee-tee). I have been awaiting your arrival for some time. I began to think that you had lost your way. As the official ambassador of the Black Hills, it is my pleasure to welcome you to his domain."

"I am pleased to meet you, Wapiti. I was not expecting to see an elk in this forest. I thought only spirit animals reside in the magical mountains."

"It is true," he responded, "that animals of the spirit world live here. But many species of wildlife call the Black Hills their home. Soon you will meet all of them. But rest now, night is upon us. You will need a suitable place to sleep. My mate and I will be honored to have you stay with us this evening. Tomorrow morning I will give you a grand tour of your new home. You will have an opportunity to meet all of the Hills' inhabitants. Come with me. Darkness is falling, it is no longer safe. Hurry, Painted Prince." And so saying, Wapiti melted into the forest.

I followed without hesitation. The handsome elk led me to a quiet birch-lined brook. There, in a bed of leaves, beneath a towering aspen, was Wapiti's lovely mate. Her soft brown eyes watched me. She smiled sweetly and invited me to join her.

Exhausted from my trip, I gratefully knelt down. Every muscle in my body began to relax. My eyelids grew heavy. Before I fell asleep, I remember hearing Wapiti's reassuring voice, "Rest peacefully, my little Prince. No harm can come to you. I will watch over you tonight."

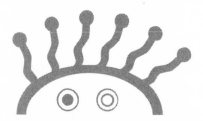

The sun, streaming through the branches, coaxed my eyes open. Once again, morning had arrived at the Great Plains. Both Wapiti and his mate were down by the brook. The big elk raised his head and proudly approached me. His imposing antlers brushed the lower branches of the trees as he passed beneath them.

"Good morning, son," Wapiti greeted. "I hope you rested well. There is much for you to do and see today. Before we begin,

I wish to give you my special gifts."

After his generosity the night before, I was overwhelmed. I told him so. "Oh, Wapiti, it is not necessary for you to give me gifts. Your hospitality is enough. No gift could be better."

"You still do not understand, little Prince. The gifts you receive are necessary; mine perhaps more than some others that have already been bestowed upon you," he said regally.

"I am Wapiti, the elk, symbol of power and absolute love. From me, you will take agility, speed, and great strength. I also give to you a heart great enough to love not only your future mate, but all the animals of the world. With my gift, you will love all of Mother Earth's creatures without reservation. You will use my strength to ensure their safety."

"Thank you, Wapiti," I said humbly. "I am truly honored. I will cherish your gifts always."

Side by side, the noble elk and I walked. He was the first to acquaint me with the magical mountains. Our time together was limited to the morning. Wapiti had many responsibilities. A migrating herd of buffalo had just arrived to spend some time in the region. Wapiti had to coordinate the welcoming committee, and make all of the necessary arrangements for the visitors.

I spent the remainder of the day exploring my beautiful new home alone. I was never really alone. I discovered many different species of animals living in the magical place. Within the eroded canyons, whitetail and mule deer would often appear, like silent silhouettes. Huge ears erect, they would stare at me with frozen curiosity. Grey and buff-colored coyotes slinked along canyon walls, their movement startling tiny chipmunks into furious circles of panic. Overhead, the darting flight of cliff swallows relieved the endless blue of a cloudless sky. Black hulks of buffalo loomed on the grasslands in the valley below, and bands of antelope dotted the nearby prairie. Cottontail rabbits scurried along well-traveled trails, while woodpeckers and chickadees busied themselves in the surrounding trees. Life was everywhere, and everywhere it welcomed me to my new home.

Mid-afternoon, I chose a high cliff on which to rest. The panorama below thrilled me. All around, the sun-warmed scent of juniper and red cedar perfumed the air. I was content and unaware of an approaching visitor.

Suddenly, a flapping of wings was followed by the image of a large bird. Before I knew it, an eagle had landed on a rock just a few feet from where I stood. A furious shaking of his tail was followed by a tucking of wings. I thought I had been astonished by the eagle's arrival, but nothing had prepared me for his brisk, spirited behavior. His voice exploded with energy, as he began to speak.

"Beautiful morning, is it not? I see that the scenery has captivated you. You should see how magnificent this land is from my point of view – high in the sky! It is a shame that horses cannot fly. Perhaps you can ask Mother Nature to rectify the situation, and give you a pair of wings," the eagle proclaimed.

"Excuse me for just one moment. I have a tail feather that is out of place! You know how it is – it drives me crazy! And look at this mess here on my chest! This will never do!" The great bird reached back to preen and fluff his shiny tail feathers and the ruffled down feathers on his chest. "Humph! There. That's better. Every feather in its place. Now. How are you doing today, Painted Prince? Oh, I'm sorry, I haven't introduced myself. I forgot that you are new to the area, and you don't know who I am yet. My name is Wambli (wahm-blee). I am the eyes in the sky for these grand hills and forests," he said proudly. It was obvious that Wambli enjoyed both his job and his position.

"I am happy to meet you, Wambli. I have heard your name before. Just the other day, Capa, the beaver, mentioned you," I said.

"Oh, yes, I was visiting there and ... and well, I was ... um, that is to say, I was checking up on you. Wapiti was so anxious about your arrival, he sent me out to see how you were doing on your journey. We couldn't have anything happen to you; you are a very special horse," the eagle responded.

"I don't understand the fuss that all the animals make over me, Wambli. And all these gifts – I hardly know what to say and do anymore. Everything seems so strange." I'm afraid my voice took on a pleading tone. I was truly mystified by what was happening to me.

"Oh," said Wambli discreetly, "you'll

learn exactly what to say and do. All in good time. And speaking of gifts, I, too, have gifts to give. To you, Painted Prince, I give the purest of hearts and the ability to run with the wind. From this day forward, I am your faithful servant. And I will be your eyes in the sky. What I see, you will see."

It was happening again, and there was nothing I could do about it. "Well, thank you, Wambli," I said uncomfortably. "How do I use these splendid gifts?"

"Why, uh, a very special creature will show you how to use all the gifts you have received. I guess the time has finally come for you to meet him," Wambli replied, equally uncomfortable.

"Who is this special creature? And where can I find him?" I asked excitedly. "I'm anxious to have everything explained to me!"

"The creature is kind of a bird. Well, not exactly an ordinary bird. Not like any bird you've ever seen before, that is. He's very large and well, he's kind of a Spirit Bird," Wambli offered.

"You mean I am to meet a bird from the spirit world? I don't think so! I mean, I'm not at all comfortable with this thing!"

Finally, I had the chance to get some answers, but I was faced with the prospect of getting them from a Spirit Bird. At the time, I didn't know what would be worse – coming face to face with a Spirit Bird or remaining ignorant!

"It's only natural to be frightened, Sky," Wambli reassured. "But once you meet Wakinyan (wah-keen-yahn) and you get past his, uh, rather unusual size and appearance, he really is quite wonderful to be around. He is wise and knowledgeable. He has been around since the beginning of time. One can learn many things listening to his tales. He is the greatest of teachers."

"You say this Spirit Bird's name is Wakinyan. What exactly does that mean, Wambli?" I asked, still apprehensive.

"Wakinyan means Thunderbird. He is the legendary Spirit Bird who flies through the sky with his eyes closed. When he flaps his massive wings, thunder booms across the land. When he opens his eyes, lightning flashes across the sky. He is not to be feared – he is a creative spirit. Wherever he appears, rain will surely follow. It is rain that keeps all of Mother Earth's creatures alive, after all," Wambli finished.

I had heard the Thunderbird flying overhead and I had seen his lightning, but I had never actually seen him. The prospect was frightening. I shared my feelings with Wambli.

"It's true. Very few animals have actually seen Wakinyan. He is extremely elusive. He reserves the right of viewing to only a select few. You, Painted Prince, are among the chosen. You will actually meet the great bird. It is time. Wakinyan is expecting you," Wambli stated.

I sensed that Wambli's order could not be refused, though I was still fearful of meeting Wakinyan. "Where will I find the Thunderbird, Wambli?" I asked.

"Do you see that great mountain yonder? Way over there? It is called Harney Peak. It is the highest point of the Black Hills. It is also the nesting place for the Thunderbird. You will find a giant cave at the summit. That is Wakinyan's home."

"But I can't climb way up there, Wambli! I'm only a horse! I don't have wings! Surely there is another way," I remarked, with some doubt.

"Oh, don't worry, Painted Prince. You have Wapiti's gift of agility, and Kela's gift of long life. No harm can come to you. The mountain has been altered by erosion. The trails are easier than they look. Besides, the Thunderbird will help if you have difficulty. Now, go on! Don't keep him waiting. This is your destiny, little Prince." Wambli opened his mighty wings and drifted out on the wind, leaving me alone.

I stood, staring up at the highest mountain I had ever seen. I wasn't sure I could climb so steep a peak. But I was a very determined brown and white spotted blue-eyed colt. I was certain that the answers to all my questions lay on Harney Peak.

CHAPTER SEVEN

It was not easy for a yearling colt to scale a mountain. My hooves slipped on the loose rock. The lichen-covered trails were narrow and steep. I struggled for what seemed like an eternity, never once looking over my shoulder. The height would have made me dizzy, and I could have lost my balance.

Slowly but surely, I moved forward and upward. The wind began to pick up. It whistled wildly around the great mountain's sides. The sky darkened and thunder shook the peak. Loose gravel and small rocks rained down upon my head and back. I leaned into the mountain side for dear life, trying to maintain my balance. I was terribly frightened!

I wondered what I was doing on the cliffs of that mountain. I was foolish to think that a horse could scale those steep granite walls.

As I inched my way along the ever narrowing ledge, I raised my head and caught sight of a large cave. Another bolt of lightning struck the mountain followed by an immense cracking sound. I quickly looked down to discover the ledge on which I was standing was crumbling beneath my hooves. Frantically, I leaped forward, barely reaching a flat boulder near the cave. My hind legs began to slip, and I envisioned falling to my death. I closed my eyes and held my breath, summoning all of my strength to scramble up out of harms way. It was a close call. I was shaken and exhausted, but I had reached the summit of Harney Peak! I shook myself vigorously to remove the dust and gravel from my spotted coat.

The cave looked very large, very dark, and very empty. I crept forward to get a closer look. I wondered where the Thunderbird could have gone. I thought he was expecting me.

Another crash of thunder rocked the mountain. The cave walls vibrated.

Lightning flashed past the mouth of the cave. The sound of wings, unlike any I had heard before, filled the air. An enormous shadow darkened the entrance to the cave.

I then, saw Wakinyan. He was perched on the ledge outside the cave entrance. He was a giant – as tall as a tree! His wingspan was longer than eight horses! The colossal bird proudly flapped his brightly-colored, iridescent wings. A deafening cry rang out from his mouth and echoed over the mountains.

The Thunderbird tucked his huge wings and lowered his head to squeeze into the cave. I stood in silence, dumfounded by the presence of the mighty bird.

He realized he was not alone. He turned his head in my direction, towering over me. I froze with fear as he stared at me with those tightly closed eyes.

"I am not alone. Who dares to enter my home without permission?" roared the Thunderbird.

Speech would not come. My vocal cords were paralyzed with fear. Eventually, I stuttered a few awkward words at the bird. "It is only me, Wakinyan. They call me the Painted Prince."

At the sound of my voice, the giant's demeanor relaxed. "You startled me, little one. I have very few visitors, but I was expecting you. I have waited for you for hundreds of years," he said thoughtfully.

"Come closer, Painted Prince, so I can get a good look at you. Indeed, you have grown up to be a fine, strong, and I might add, handsome, colt. I am very proud of you, as is the rest of the animal kingdom."

I felt uneasy approaching the Thunderbird. I noticed that he always kept his eyes closed and did not turn toward me when I spoke, though his voice was confident and reassuring. The face of the Wakinyan displayed wisdom and understanding. Gradually, wonder and curiosity replaced my fear. I drew closer to the giant bird and listened intently to his words.

Sensing my nearness, he again began to speak. "I'm sure your short life has been difficult. You must have many questions for me. That is why you are here, Painted Prince. You were born a horse of a different color for a reason.

"The Black Hills became your friend. You have met animals who have presented you with their special powers. These, too, are for a reason. You, my son, were chosen by Mother Earth to complete a very difficult task.

"Hear me now. I am Wakinyan, Lord of Thunder and Lightning, Keeper of the Truth. I am here to answer your questions and to teach you the secrets of the Great Plains.

"In order to receive these gifts, little Prince, you need to open your eyes, your ears, and your heart. You must be willing to learn and accept the responsibilities of this sacred knowledge. You must treasure and use it wisely. You must be aware that in possessing this knowledge, you will encounter many challenges in your lifetime. You must be strong and wise enough to overcome these obstacles.

"For the rest of your life, you will be charged with maintaining the balance and harmony of the universe. Do you understand and accept your destiny, little Prince?" the Wakinyan concluded.

Finally, I began to comprehend what it was all about – the spots and blue eyes that had set me apart, the recognition, the gifts. I was astonished and somewhat relieved. With this insight, my life began to take on new meaning and purpose.

And, so it was. On that day, and without hesitation, I agreed to become Sunka Wakan, the Great Spirit Horse.

CHAPTER EIGHT

For three years I was the Thunderbird's student. Time passed quickly. I grew to love the great bird. He became a friend as well as a mentor.

There were times when I longed to be with my family herd, but they were infrequent. The Thunderbird kept me busy with my lessons. The wonderful animals of the sacred mountains became my friends and occupied much of my free time with their stories and games.

In Wakinyan's cave, great changes had taken place in me. I found an inner peace that I had never known. I was more confident and more at ease with myself. For the first time in my life, I was genuinely happy.

Physical changes had also taken place in those three years. Gone was the gangling yearling. I had grown much taller. By the time I was four, I had attained a height of 15.2 hands. My body had matured, becoming muscular and strong. The short, fuzzy mane and tail of my youth had been replaced by long, silky hair that floated as I ran, much as I remembered the mane and tail of my father.

And yes, I was still brown and white spotted with blue eyes. But I had become a stallion.

One morning, at the close of those three years, I prepared for my daily race with Tate (tah-tay), the Wind. It was one of those magical Black Hills mornings. I stood on Harney Peak and challenged Tate to a great race. He obliged, as always. That day, he came whistling around the mountain walls, picking up speed at every turn, in the hope of beating me. I waited patiently until I felt him rush past me. Off we went!

Down, down the narrow trails of the peak we barreled. Across the rocky hills, dashing into the forest, dodging in and out of giant pines, we headed towards the valley below. In the heavily treed obstacle course, I was always several feet behind my opponent. But as soon as we entered the high grass, making a sharp turn towards the lake, I called upon my special powers. I then galloped effortlessly across the finish line and defeated Tate. I reared skyward in victory, whinnying at my friend. He acknowledged his defeat by circling me furiously then disappearing. It was his way of showing self-disgust. Oh, how I loved to challenge the Wind!

High up on Harney Peak, Wambli the eagle visited the Thunderbird. The pair often watched my escapades. They talked quietly as I climbed up the mountain. I wondered if they knew how much of their conversation I overheard.

"He has certainly grown into a fine stallion, hasn't he, Wakinyan? And the way he handles my gift! Why, he would make any eagle envious. So many wonderful changes have taken place in him these past few years," I heard Wambli muse.

"Great changes have indeed occurred, Wambli," Wakinyan admitted. "We have witnessed his transformation from an awkward yearling into Sunka Wakan, the Great Spirit Horse. I regret that the time has come for him to leave the Black Hills. There is nothing left for me to teach him. He needs to use what he has learned. Mother Earth awaits her new King."

Wambli's voice grew sad. "Gee, I hate to see him go. We will miss him terribly. I sense that you will experience a bit of the 'empty nest syndrome' soon," Wambli continued.

"What you say is true, Wambli. I have grown very fond of the horse. His presence will be deeply missed. But he has a higher calling. Not even I can keep him from his destiny. Remember, Wambli, he will take a part of each of us with him. We will never really be separated. That should be some consolation," his voice trailed off, as he heard me approach.

"He's coming now. Will you excuse us? I need to speak to Sunka Wakan in private," Wakinyan asked.

I watched Wambli take flight just as I climbed to the cliff's edge, where the Thunderbird perched, waiting in silence. As he gazed over the valley with his eyes tightly closed, I sensed something different about the great Spirit Bird. He seemed preoccupied; a look of sadness clouded his face. There was something I had never seen before in his expression.

Wanting to postpone the inevitable parting as long as possible, I attempted to engage him in light conversation. "Did you see how I raced Tate, Wakinyan? Gosh, I really humiliated him in that race. I could have crossed the finish line even sooner if it were not for a rock. I picked one up in my left, rear hoof when I crossed that far hill over there," I concluded, looking east.

The sadness I saw on Wakinyan's face gave way to a look of regret. The Thunderbird had something to say, and nothing I did would prevent him from saying it.

"You were wonderful, son. The Wind is very foolish, indeed, if he thinks that he can beat you in a race. But come now, I need you near me. I have something very important to discuss with you.

"You have done well with all your lessons these past three years. I am proud of you. But my role as your teacher is now over. You know all the secrets of the Great

Plains. It is time for you to leave the Black Hills

"There is much more for you to see and do. You will not accomplish anything further by remaining here, even though I would like you to stay. You need to take all that has been given to you, and taught to you, where it is needed most – out there on the Great Plains. They are your kingdom. You must rule over your entire realm, not just the Black Hills."

I was shaken by the Thunderbird's words, though in truth I knew that day would eventually come. I tried to control the tears that were filling my eyes.

"Thunderbird, I do not want to leave you and all my dear friends. You know how much I love the Black Hills. I am happy here. You cannot ask me to leave the place where my heart is," I replied, with great feeling.

"Long ago I explained this to you, my son. You will have to make some sacrifices to become the Keeper of the Plains' secrets. You will never realize your role as the Great Spirit Horse unless you take the sacred knowledge and apply it to your new life. That life will begin on this very day – at this very moment.

"You have received many gifts. Now, before you go, I wish to give you my special gift. I saved it for this moment.

"No gift will be as important to you as mine. You must treat it with great respect. You must use it carefully and wisely. It is a gift no mere mortal animal could ever use.

"You have never once questioned me about my eyes. They must remain closed if I am to retain my great power. Only in the fury of a storm will I open my eyes. Then, I release upon Mother Earth my supernatural strength.

"My special gift to you is lightning. All these years I could not open my eyes in your presence. I feared that my powerful lightning would harm you. Now, you are the Great Spirit Horse. You have earned the right to command my gift," Wakinyan promised.

The Thunderbird turned to face me. He lowered his head and slowly began to open his huge eyes. They glowed brightly, like burning embers. He urged me to look into their fiery depths.

"Do not be afraid, Sunka Wakan. Gaze into my eyes. You are about to witness what no other living creature has ever experienced. Look into the world of creative storms. Feel their energy. Capture my lightning. It is now yours!" The great bird began to flap his wings. Thunder rolled across the mountaintop.

I continued staring into his eyes, fixed upon the raging storm within. Suddenly a bolt of lightning exploded from the Thunderbird's glowing eyes into mine! I fell back, blinded. Intense heat surged through my head. My knees gave way. The heat continued to pulsate, traveling throughout my body.

Then the Thunderbird closed his eyes. He must have moved forward to help me, because the heat began to recede, and my vision returned. Still shaky, I managed to stand with his help.

"You will be fine in a few moments," I heard Wakinyan say, as though from a great distance. "That was a powerful bolt of lightning. You handled it well. Now, it is yours to keep. Take it with you, for it is time to go.

"You take a part of me, as well as many others, on your journey. We will always be with you. This is the beginning of your adventure as Sunka Wakan, the Great Spirit Horse. I will say farewell to the others for you, my son. Go in peace."

"Wakinyan, you have been like a father to me. I can't put into words my feelings ... I can't leave you ... I ... "

"I know of your love and gratitude, son. Now, it is time for you to leave," he said firmly.

As I turned to leave Harney Peak, the Spirit Bird turned as well, hiding his face from my view. I could hear his teardrops raining softly on the ledge where he perched. Slowly, I made my way down from the summit and approached the forest's edge. For a moment, I stopped on the top of a large, flat rock and gazed out into the vastness of the plains.

It was painful for me to leave the magical mountains. But the Thunderbird was right – I had become a stallion. The time had come for me to take responsibility for the life I chose to lead.

I had learned much in those three years from my friend, the Black Hills, and all of his inhabitants. The Wakinyan had been a dedicated teacher. I was well prepared for my role. The harmony of Mother Earth depended upon me. I was confident that I could be a wise and noble ruler – the one needed to protect her.

On that day, for the first time, I, Sunka Wakan, the Great Spirit Horse, stepped out onto the Great Plains and claimed my kingdom.

CHAPTER NINE

I chose to head northwest on my new adventure. In the distance I first saw Mato Tipi (mah-toe-tee-pee), also known as Grizzly Bear's Lodge. This brilliant monument was unique to the plains. Looming large over the hills and grasslands as it did, Mato Tipi covered some one thousand feet at its base and nearly two acres across its summit. It was visible for many miles.

I often watched Mato Tipi from my refuge in the Black Hills, its appearance ever changing in the shifting light. One moment it looked dark and brooding, the next it was transformed into a brilliant beacon. It's air of beauty and mystery enticed me, and so did the story told by the Wakinyan.

According to the Thunderbird, the fluted rock of Mato Tipi resulted from the scratching of bears' claws. Long ago seven human girls were attacked by bears. To save them, the Great Spirit elevated a rock on which they had huddled, far from the reach of the bears. That rock became Mato Tipi; the clawing of the bears became the fluted striations that run up and down the rock. The bears never reached the girls, and they died from the exhaustion of their efforts. The Great Spirit then plucked the seven maidens from the summit of Mato Tipi and gave them a permanent home in the heavens, where they became seven stars of the evening sky.

My decision was easy to make. Mato Tipi was to be my very first destination.

To hasten my trip, I called upon my friend, the Wind. He descended quickly from the swirling clouds, ever ready to serve me.

"Take it easy, Tate," I cautioned him, "this is the first time you will be serving me in this way."

He replied with a sharp whistle, positioning himself carefully around each of my hooves. I signaled him with a nod and bolted forward in full gallop.

Every stride I took was accompanied by Tate moving in unison with me. The sound of my hoofbeats disappeared. I was no longer traveling upon the earth, but through the air above it. The power of the Wind carried me at incredible speeds across the desolate prairie. I found my gift from Wambli truly exhilarating! My own great speed, increased by Tate, made me the fastest living creature on Mother Earth.

We arrived at Mato Tipi in no time at all. The Wind carefully lowered me to the ground, ruffled my forelock, and bade me goodbye. I thanked him for speeding me on my journey.

It was a peaceful and wondrous place. Immediately, I felt at home. Mato Tipi, I could see, was in reality a mighty pillar of once-molten rock. Thrusting into the prairie sky, it left a powerful image in my mind. It was a place of austere and serene beauty.

Barren rocks gave way to a succession of colorful plants and waving trees. A calm, blue river flowed gracefully along the base of Mato Tipi, softening the landscape. A multitude of life lived around, and gathered to, the imposing rock tower.

I drank with no fear of the Unktehi, confident that he was sleeping soundly in so tranquil an environment. As I drank, I noticed a buff-colored coyote slinking along the riverbank. It was a large, scraggly looking individual. His beady eyes examined me. A sly, crooked grin spread across his face as he approached. The coyote sat down beside me, casually licking his paw, his expression never changing.

"What brings you to Mato Tipi, Great Spirit Horse?" his voice hissed. "I wasn't aware that any special occasion was imminent."

"I don't believe we've met, coyote," I responded hesitantly.

"No, not exactly. We haven't exactly met," he said, and again I noted the crafty look he wore and the rasping whine of his voice.

"All of the animals living here know about you," he continued. "My name is Miyaca (me-yah-cha), cha, cha, cha. To be honest, I am not particularly fond of horses, even if they are Great Spirit Horses. This is my territory. Why did you choose to come to my home? Are you hoping for another gift?"

"I have already been blessed with many gifts, Miyaca. I didn't know I could receive additional powers, and I am not so sure I would want more, if they were offered." Something in the coyote's tone and posture offended me. I'm sure my own conveyed my displeasure.

"Soooo, the Thunderbird didn't tell you. That doesn't surprise me one bit. After all, everyone knows that he despises the Unktehi. Why would he want you to possess the water creature's great gift?" Miyaca winked.

"What are you talking about, Miyaca?" I said, clearly annoyed.

It was obvious that Miyaca enjoyed the effect his words had on me. With the air of a conspirator, he began to turn in ever smaller circles, creating a comfortable nest. He stretched out on the ground, crossed his front legs, and continued his story.

"Well ... since the Spirit Bird neglected to inform you, I guess I will have to tell you about this greatest of powers. You see, many, many years ago the Thunderbird was extremely jealous of all the attention Mother Earth gave to her two special creations, the water creatures. That's right, Spirit Horse," Miyaca emphasized, sensing my disbelief. "Long ago, there were two Unktehi. Both brothers ruled well. They protected the waters that flowed across Mother Earth's body.

"The Thunderbird felt very slighted by being given only the sky to rule. His hurt grew to resentment. Resentment grew into real hatred. One day, without warning, the Thunderbird killed one of the young Unktehi. It's true. He burnt the Unktehi to a crisp with his lightning bolts. The poor creature's bones are all that remain, disintegrating into the landscape that we now call the Badlands," Miyaca finished smugly.

"I don't understand why the Wakinyan withheld this information, Miyaca. And I can't imagine that wise bird being capable of jealousy, let alone murder," I responded, somewhat heatedly.

"Why do you think he lives in solitude on Harney Peak? When you arrived he was careful to hide the truth. He feared you would seek to gain the Unktehi's great gift. Doing so would make you more powerful even than the Thunderbird, himself. Unktehi's strength would enable you to punish the Spirit Bird and avenge the death of the Unktehi's brother. That is your true destiny, Spirit Horse. You must correct this terrible injustice and reveal the truth about the Thunderbird," the coyote demanded.

"I must hear both sides of the story to make a proper judgement, Miyaca. I will first speak to the Unktehi. How do I summon him?" I asked.

"To begin with, you must wake the water creature. I know for a fact that he has been waiting for you for a very long time. He has expressed to me, personally, his great desire to gift you with his supernatural powers. He will no doubt welcome you with open arms. Just wade across his watery body, and you will meet your new, best friend," Miyaca advised.

It sounded too easy. But what was I to do? I had to get to the heart of Miyaca's story. At the time, it seemed to me, it was necessary to confront the Unktehi.

I approached the riverbank and cautiously placed one hoof into the water. It was icy cold. I hesitated briefly, but I had to know the truth. Proceeding with great care, ever so slowly, I waded into the river. It's muddy bed dropped off unexpectedly, forcing me to swim. The once calm river began to swirl, and I found myself nearly submerged in icy water. The current accelerated and grew in intensity, tugging furiously at my legs. Waves of white water splashed wildly across my face, making it difficult for me to keep my head above water.

I was halfway across the river, but I was struggling for my life. Fearing death, I summoned Capa's gift. Immediately, my body became more buoyant, and great physical strength coursed through my legs. My hooves drove me through the raging water like huge paddles. With my head completely submerged, I found that I could hold my breath for a prolonged period of time. Confidence overwhelmed me. I suddenly felt like a great brown and white spotted blue-eyed fish!

Just as I reached the shoreline, an enormous wave of water swelled skyward, revealing the fearsome image of Unktehi, the legendary water monster. In the sunlight his towering body seemed to glisten with fury. His sinister blue eyes searched the shoreline for the intruder who had interrupted his sleep.

"Who dares to disturb Unktehi from his

sound sleep?" his voice exploded. "Who dares to defy the ancient rules? When Mother Earth created me, my rules were firmly established. Who challenges them? Could it be you, little horse? You challenge my fluid greatness?" he asked disdainfully.

There was no way to describe the Unktehi's voice. I recall that it was so deep, so resonant, that it seemed to thunder into my very soul. Without avail, I flattened my ears to relieve the vibrations pulsating within my eardrums.

"I am the Great Spirit Horse, Unktehi," I replied with some apprehension. "I regret disturbing your sleep. Miyaca, the coyote, advised that you wished to speak to me and present me with a special gift. There is also another matter, that needs your clarification. For both of these reasons, I woke you." He seemed to consider my words, but I could detect no relenting in his attitude towards me when he spoke.

"Like yourself, Miyaca is a pesky land animal. He is also a trickster and a liar. Only fools listen to his words. Surely, as the 'Great Spirit Horse,' you know this," he said with contempt.

"I never had a desire to speak to you,

and I never will. Since you have summoned me, I will give you a special gift. For defying my rules, I give you the gift of death! Death to you and all living creatures on Mother Earth! The time has come to destroy all of you. As you watch the destruction, horse, remember that you, and you alone, have caused my fury. I will start with the very thing that you love most, your family herd. I happen to know that they are grazing in one of your father's favorite box canyons, not far from here. How convenient! There is no place for them to run. No escape. They will all drown. I will provide their watery grave," he gurgled gleefully.

"Now, watch my body grow and grow. Watch as I become the greatest flood that the Great Plains has ever experienced. Nothing can stop me. When I am finished, there will be no life on Mother Earth. There will be only my huge body, over all the earth. How glorious! Ha, ha, ha, ha ha!"

The monster grew to a height so enormous that I could no longer see his eyes. His body swelled so that it seemed to fill the horizon. Then began the churning and bubbling, and the destruction of everything in his path. I leaped onto a large rock before his waters engulfed me, as well. It was horrifying.

I thought, what had I done? I had allowed myself to be tricked by the coyote. I was the ruler of the Great Plains for less than a day and had already inspired the destruction of my own kingdom.

The entire animal world was dependent upon my protection. The lessons of the great Thunderbird were all for naught. My gifts were worthless, because I did not possess the wisdom to use them.

In despair, I recalled the lullaby my mother had once sung to me. It had celebrated my future greatness and destiny as the Great Spirit Horse. I wondered if she realized then that she and the rest of the herd would be destroyed by the very one upon whom they relied for protection. I had failed miserably. I felt unworthy to bear the name Sunka Wakan. Who was I to stop the devastating floodwaters of Unktehi? I was, after all, only a brown and white spotted blue-eyed horse.

I must have given voice to these thoughts. Instantly, I heard a familiar sound.

"A true king does not speak in this manner. When things become difficult, a real king does not give up."

I was so surprised to hear that voice that I almost fell from the rock on which I stood. My head turned upward in the direction from which it came. I couldn't believe my eyes. There, high above the stormy water, was the old grizzly, Mato. He found safety seated upon a large outcropping of Mato Tipi. Although, he looked little worse for the chaos around him.

"Mato!" I cried, "What are you doing here? Are you safe?"

"Of course, I am safe, Spirit Horse! And why wouldn't I be here? After all, this is my home. Why do you think it is called Mato Tipi? But enough of that now. It looks like you need my help. Listen to me, Spirit Horse. You cannot give up after your first mistake. It is part of the learning process. You will continue to make mistakes – Mother Earth willing – throughout your life. Confronting them is the first step. You must forgive yourself and take responsibility. The animals of the world and the Thunderbird need to trust you. We must all have faith. You are not entirely to blame. The coyote lied to you. Because you are pure of heart, you believed him. In seeking the truth you made two mistakes. You did not heed your instincts, and you did not trust the great power of Kimi Mila. If you had, you would have been able to detect the danger in Miyaca's words. Do you wish to know the truth, Spirit Horse?" Mato began, "In the beginning ... "

Just as Mato started his tale, my attention was diverted by the flapping of wings and screeching cry of an eagle. It was Wambli, flying high above. From the exasperated look on his face, I could see he intended to call a halt to Mato's recital.

"Not now, Mato!" the eagle abruptly exclaimed, as he circled directly overhead. "In case you haven't noticed, Unktehi is well on his way to annihilating the Great Plains. Sunka Wakan, your family will be among the first to go, unless we get there ahead of the Unktehi. Summon Tate to you immediately! I will fly along and tell you the tale, myself."

Wambli's words brought Mato and I back to the urgent situation at hand.

"Find a safe place now, Mato. I go to stop the Unktehi!" I called.

"I will be fine. Sunka Wakan is protecting me!" Mato replied with feeling.

Once again, I called the Wind to my aid. Hearing the urgency in my voice, he quickly flew down, positioned himself around my hooves, and awaited my command.

"Speed is vital, my friend. Today, we are not playing. I need your gale-force strength. I must stop the Unktehi before he reaches my family! Let's go!"

I bolted forward, and Tate carried my galloping body upward at incredible speed. We were well out of the reach of the water monster's angry swells. Nearby flew Wambli, still wearing a look of grave anxiety.

"Turn south, Tate, I know a shortcut over the bluffs up ahead. We can still reach the canyon in time," Wambli commanded him.

"Now, horse, you must hear this story. I will tell you what really happened, not the story Miyaca would have you believe," Wambli said, as he flew alongside Tate and me. At last another important secret of the plains was about to be revealed to me – the reason behind the Unktehi's unquenchable rage.

CHAPTER TEN

Just as Wambli, Tate, and I began to gain speed, I heard another sound. Over the the crashing water and whirling wind came a plaintive call for help.

"Help me, help me! Please! Somebody save me. I'm drowning. Please help me!" a voice cried.

Searching the waters below I spotted Miyaca, clinging desperately to a log which tossed him to and fro in the waters of Unktehi.

"Oh, Great Spirit Horse! Please save me! I am a poor swimmer. Don't let Unktehi drown me!" he begged.

Although Miyaca had, at least in part, caused the destruction at hand, I couldn't let him drown. After all, I was the

champion of all of Mother Earth's
creatures, even those who were unworthy.
I looked to Wambli for confirmation. He
acknowledged with a grim nod. I slowed
Tate and turned my attention to Miyaca.

"Hang on, Miyaca, I'm coming. But first
you must make a solemn promise. You
must never again lie to or trick another
living creature. Not for the remainder of
your life. Do you swear to give up your
deceitful and evil ways, Miyaca?" I
demanded.

"Can't you see I'm drowning here?" he
hissed. "I have water in my ears, and I can
barely hear you. I have swallowed an
ocean of water, and I can hardly speak
from exhaustion. I am not capable of
giving you an answer."

"Then you'll have to fend for yourself,
coyote. My business is too urgent to stop
and haggle with you. I'll check to see if you
are among the living later this evening," I
responded.

"Wait! Don't go. I promise, Great Spirit
Horse, that I will never lie again. Now
please! Please help me," he whined. With
that, the Wind took me down to Miyaca.
We hovered directly over the whimpering
coyote, and I signaled him to grasp my tail

with his mouth. Having secured himself thus, Tate and I swept him to a nearby rock formation jutting high above the floodwaters. There we set the waterlogged Miyaca down.

"You are safe for now, Miyaca. I must be on my way to stop further destruction."

"Stay with me, Spirit Horse. The water monster may try to drown me again. Don't leave me alone! Don't leave me!" he pleaded pitifully.

"You will be fine for now, Miyaca. Remember your promise. I, Sunka Wakan, will insure your safety unless, of course, you fail to keep that promise," I replied.

Looking out across the horizon I could see nothing but the Unktehi's raging waters. I had spent enough time with Miyaca. I had to leave immediately or risk losing others. Wambli's increasingly anxious look confirmed this.

"Tate, we must hurry, now! Take me to the box canyon and my family herd!" I urged. "Wambli, tell your tale with all haste. I must understand the Unktehi's rage before I can take appropriate action to stop him," I said, turning quickly to the eagle.

I was fearful. I hoped that in saving Miyaca I had not lost the opportunity to save my family. The thought propelled me onward. I used all the strength given to me by Mato and Wapiti. Tate responded with hurricane-force strength of his own. Wambli spoke as we flew.

"In the beginning, Sunka Wakan, Mother Earth did create two Unktehi. Both hated the Thunderbird. They were jealous of his lightning. They were jealous because all living creatures worshiped the Spirit Bird's power to bring life-giving rain. Above all, they resented the Thunderbird because his thunderstorms nourished their bodies. They needed the Thunderbird as much as everyone else did! Without his rains, the two Unktehi would suffer drought in dry weather. But the Thunderbird gladly gave the rain to the Unktehi. They were ingrates! And so, the two Unktehi plotted to do away with all living creatures, and take over Mother Earth with their water. They began to create devastating floods. Naturally, the Thunderbird was quite alarmed. Unable to reason with the two monsters, he had no choice but to destroy them. He sent down blazing lightning bolts to consume the floodwaters. One of the Unktehi was destroyed in the process. His bones still rest amid the Badlands, his fossil remains serving as a reminder of the evil and terror wrought by the Unktehi. The Thunderbird spared the remaining Unktehi, and forced the creature to abide by Mother Earth's Rules – or else. The Spirit Bird has never been the same from that day until this. Grief stricken and full of guilt, he remains in seclusion on Harney Peak. Though he had done the only thing possible under the circumstances, he has never forgiven himself. The Thunderbird vowed never to take the life of a spirit creature again, regardless of the situation," Wambli explained.

"What did I do to enrage the Unktehi, Wambli?" I called across the sky.

"Nothing. It is of no importance. It was only a matter of time before this Unktehi would seek to avenge his brother's death. Your arrival was just an excuse. Once again, he is attempting to destroy Mother Earth's creatures. You possess the power to stop this destruction. But you must believe in yourself, Spirit Horse. You have been chosen to champion the creatures of Mother Earth. You are the only one who can stop the Unktehi," Wambli proclaimed finally.

"Must I destroy the water monster to do so, Wambli?" I wondered.

"The time for questions is over, Spirit Horse. Trust your instincts," declared the eagle.

Over the churning waves and spray I could see the box canyon ahead and hear the distant cries of panic-stricken horses. The time for action had arrived.

Tate swept me past Unktehi's writhing body. He set me down at the canyon mouth mere moments before the water monster arrived. Wambli continued to fly overhead, watching and waiting.

Amidst the chaos, my presence went unnoticed. Every horse wore a look of terror. Some were trying vainly to climb the canyon walls. Others huddled together in small groups awaiting their fate. My father raced back and forth trying to maintain order and calm the herd. I sensed his desperation. Positioning myself directly in Unktehi's path, I blocked the water monster's access to the canyon.

The Unktehi continued to advance toward the canyon and the helpless horses within it. Just before he reached me,

Unktehi abruptly changed direction and reared upwards, forming a terrifying tower of living water. Behind me, the family herd stopped in their panic. Paralyzed with fear, they stared at the colossal creature that towered over the walls of the canyon.

"Why, if it isn't the Great Spirit Horse again," Unktehi rumbled. "I had no idea you wanted to watch the drowning of your family. You make everything extremely convenient; for you are to be included among my victims. Now, move out of my way, horse!" he roared.

I stood my ground.

"Hold where you are, Unktehi. I have had enough of your evil doings. I am here to stop you, and I will destroy you if I must."

"How could you possibly stop me?" Unktehi sneered.

"Obviously you are not aware of my powers, water monster. I possess the strength of a grizzly." To demonstrate, I turned and lashed out at a large boulder, sending it directly towards Unktehi. Not to be outdone, the monster tossed the boulder aside as though it were a mere pebble.

"You'll have to do better than that,

Spirit Horse! Remember, I can drown a grizzly bear, even a very strong one. In fact, why don't I just drown you here and now?" Unktehi responded.

"You cannot drown me, Unktehi. I possess the power of the beaver. I am the strongest swimmer on Mother Earth," I asserted.

"Well then, horse, when I am finished here, you will have an entire universe to prove that! You will swim for all eternity. There will be no land left for you to walk upon. Unless you learn to eat fish, you will starve, foolish horse," Unktehi bellowed.

"You leave me no choice, Unktehi. I must destroy you. I possess a power no mortal animal ever shall. The Wakinyan has given me his supernatural abilities. Yes, Unktehi – I, Sunka Wakan, possess the power to control lightning!" I shouted.

I could feel the frenzy of the storm building within me. My blue eyes changed dramatically, revealing the seething black skies of an approaching thunderstorm. As they darkened, sparks of light flashed across their stormy centers, making them glow a fiery red. A tremendous burst of lightning exploded forth from my eyes, striking the ground only inches from the water monster's flowing base.

"Do you doubt me, Unktehi? There's more where that came from. I do not wish to destroy you. You are one of Mother Earth's most wondrous creations. But I will do so if you continue your current course," I assured him.

A bubbling tremor in his body seemed to indicate a change in Unktehi. I believed that he was finally taking me seriously.

"Well, ahem, there is no need to over-react," his voice gurgled soothingly. "It is well known that I have an aversion for lightning. I have no desire to meet the same fate as did my brother. Perhaps we can bargain a bit, eh, Spirit Horse?"

"There is no bargain! It is my way or no way, Unktehi. Calm your waters now! Heed what I have to say," I demanded.

Recognizing the truth of my powers, Unktehi began to shrink and retreat. His angry white waters stopped churning. His fluid face took on a look of obedient, wide-eyed innocence. Still, I remained watchful. I knew it was unwise to trust the water monster.

"Mother Earth created you and relies on you to keep her creations alive and well," I began sternly. "I do not understand your

anger, but even if I did, I know it would not
warrant the destruction of all living
things. They have done nothing wrong.
For centuries they have faithfully
worshiped you. When they drink of you, or
swim in you, or make their homes in you,
they become a part of you, and you of
them. By destroying these creatures you
are destroying a part of yourself. Nature
needs you. Not only for your life-
sustaining waters, but for your
exceptional beauty. That beauty is
essential to life on Mother Earth. Your
peaceful ponds, serene lakes and streams,
mighty rivers, spectacular waterfalls, and
majestic oceans each bring joy to those
who look upon them. Without your beauty
our lives would be empty and barren. I
need your help, too, Unktehi," I said at
last, watching his reaction. "I need you to
continue to ensure the well-being of all of
nature and to enrich the lives of all with
your beauty. It is true that I am the ruler
of the Great Plains. But you, my friend,
are the noble ruler of the water. Two wise
and powerful kings should combine forces
to maintain the balance and harmony of
the universe."

I could see Unktehi's color softening.

I could feel the warming of his body. My words seemed to have their desired effect, and I waited for his response.

"Spirit Horse," he said with genuine warmth, "I begin to see this situation in a different light. I may have been a bit hasty in my actions. It is obvious that I am a wise and noble king, and, as you say, surpassingly beautiful, in a handsome sort of way, that is. You are right about my subjects. They are many and faithful. They worship me. After all, who would I rule if I destroyed all these living things? I don't think I should dilly-dally here any longer. There are too many relying on my precious water. I have much to plan and do. In fact, I must decide immediately whether to wear a great crown of shells or an emerald robe of algae ... or maybe I should create a new river or ocean. My subjects expect something spectacular, as befits a king of my stature, you know," he mused, completely absorbed in reflections of his own grandeur.

"I will consider your offer, Spirit Horse. But now, I really must go. As king, there is so much to do, and so little time in which to do it," he trailed off, retreating in spirit as well as body from the canyon.

I watched as Unktehi receded and returned the plains to their normal state. Wambli stopped circling and followed Unktehi's retreat. It seemed, for the moment that the monster was satisfied by my reminder of his essential role on Mother Earth. I knew it would not be the last time Unktehi's anger would be released. He was vain and fickle. When another outbreak of watery temper occurred, I was confident that Sunka Wakan would be ready and waiting.

I thought of my family standing nearby. It had been three years since I had seen them – three years and one near disaster. I wondered what would we have to say to one another.

CHAPTER ELEVEN

I wheeled around to face my family. They stared at me in silence, as they often had when I was a yearling, but their stares were filled with wonder rather than disdain. I looked them over, counting each familiar face, relieved to see everyone had survived unharmed.

Finally, the silence was broken by the sound of my father's hooves trotting toward me. He was still the majestic figure of my colthood, but I could immediately see a difference in his attitude toward me. I waited for him to speak first.

"Sky! It is so wonderful to see you! Your mother and I have missed you so much. Are you well? Why, of course you are! Just look at you! You are a stallion now, and I have seen with my own eyes that you are a wise and noble stallion, worthy of the title Great Spirit Horse.

"I am grateful to you for coming to the rescue of the family herd. You are a hero now, Sky, Mother Earth's greatest hero. And mine, too. I am so proud of you!" he said, deeply moved.

"I am happy to see you, too, Father. It has, indeed, been a long time. I have changed in many ways, yet I am still a brown and white spotted blue-eyed horse. And you are, and always will be, my hero, Father. That will never change," I responded with equal warmth.

"Well, you know, Sky," he continued in a choked voice, "I have never been good at putting my feelings into words. I have always wanted to say, well, I just had to tell you that ... I love you, Sky." He nickered in amusement at his confession.

"And will you look at me," he added, "I'm still calling you Sky! I see that I'm going to have some difficulty with your new name and title, Sunka Wakan, the Great Spirit Horse."

"You don't have to call me Sky, the Painted Prince, Sunka Wakan, or the Great Spirit Horse. Just call me Son.

That's all I ever wanted. I love you, Father," I said affectionately.

It was a magical moment between a father and his son. I held it close to my heart for many years. For the first time Raven, the legendary black stallion and my father, lowered his head and gently touched my nose with his own. Tears of joy ran from his ebony eyes. Another silence fell upon the herd as we bonded in the canyon, father and son.

The magic was short-lived, however. We were abruptly interrupted by my mother's voice.

"Well, can't a mother say hello to her only son?" she inquired sweetly.

There she was. Her perfect white star shined as brightly as her brown eyes. Without words, I stepped forward and caressed my mother's neck. Her wonderful scent filled my head and my heart with fond childhood memories. At that moment, I realized just how much I had missed my parents.

The family herd drew closer to the three of us, basking in the warmth of our reunion. Gratitude, relief, and curiosity played equally across their faces. Yet, they stood waiting for a word or gesture, to signal invitation to our conversation.

"Of course you will be staying with the family herd now, Son," Raven told me. "I am getting on in years. I could use your help. I was hoping someday you would become the leader of the herd. As the Great Spirit Horse, you could keep the family safe. We would truly flourish with your leadership."

"I hate to disappoint you, Father, but the peace and harmony of our family is only part of what I must attend to. My responsibility extends to the entire universe. My obligations are far reaching. I hope you and Mother will understand. It would be impossible for me to remain here," I explained.

The disappointment that spread across my father's face was quickly replaced by acceptance. It was my mother who reestablished the connection between us.

"Say no more, Son," she said, "I have always known that you were the chosen one. I understand your higher calling. The family will be just fine. Besides," she added, winking at my father, "your Father still has plenty of kick left in him. He will be a strong leader for many years to come."

A sense of peace and resolution grew among us – my Mother, my Father, and myself. We each smiled and nodded our heads in acceptance.

Our reunion was ultimately interrupted by the impatient approach of one of the family herd. A mare was trying to get our attention by pawing softly at the ground. When I looked her way my eyes were filled with the vision of a magnificent chestnut. Her long, flowing red mane and tail glistened in the sunlight. Her eyes sparkled with joy. She moved gracefully, her strong, sleek body coming closer and closer.

Eventually, I noticed the perfect heart-shaped snip on the end of her nose. It was White Heart, my sweet and timid childhood friend! The years had made great changes in her as well. She was no longer a little filly. Time had transformed White Heart into an exquisite mare.

"Son, you remember White Heart, don't you?" my father asked, breaking an awkward silence.

"I remember White Heart, Father. I could not forget her. She was always kind to me when we were ... when we were young. I have missed you, White Heart,"

I said, giving the mare my full attention.

"It is wonderful to see you again. I am sorry you will not be staying with the herd," White Heart said, with regret. Do you remember the request I made of you three years ago?" she continued, haltingly. " I asked a brown and white spotted, blue-eyed colt, named Sky, if I could join him on his journey. He politely told me no. He said it was too dangerous. I never saw that colt again. Today, I am asking Sunka Wakan, the Great Spirit Horse, a similar question," she stated eloquently. "May I join you on your journey to greatness?"

I was speechless. Was I to consider White Heart's offer? I looked to my father for guidance. His wink was all the approval I needed. I turned back to White Heart and looked directly into her beaming brown eyes. The words I spoke to her on that day changed my life forever.

"Will you come with me, White Heart? Beside Sunka Wakan you will always be safe. And I can promise you a life full of adventure. The Great Spirit Horse would be honored to share the rest of his life with you," I said with pride.

White Heart moved to my side and bowed her head. In watching her approach

I noticed the herd at large, around her.

I hadn't realized that they had gathered closer, listening to our conversation. Suddenly, they began rearing skyward, whinnying and cheering. The joy and acceptance of the herd was overwhelming, a welcome change from their earlier criticism.

My father waited until the herd had quieted before trying to speak. Proudly, he addressed them.

"Meet the new King and leader of the plains. This is my son, Sunka Wakan, the Great Spirit Horse! Beside him is his chosen Queen, White Heart!"

The rejoicing spread throughout the Great Plains. Birds, and beasts alike joined in the celebration, and Mother Earth sang her ancient song of peace and harmony.

Far away in the distance I could see the smiling face of the Black Hills. Against the colors of a setting sun, his majestic silhouette watched and waited. It was time for me to return to my home. I bade the herd farewell. Once again, I, the Great Spirit Horse, galloped across my beloved plains. I was heading home, with my queen, to my magical mountain range.

EPILOGUE

The years passed quickly. I experienced many exciting adventures as the Great Spirit Horse. White Heart always accompanied me; we were inseparable.

As much as we enjoyed the high adventure, we looked forward to the peaceful times, when harmony was restored to Mother Earth.

During those times, we would visit the family herd. My father, Raven, was still their noble leader. His ebony mane was streaked with silver, a tribute to his age and great wisdom. Star Face, my mother, was just as beautiful as ever and, as ever, stood by my father's side.

I even enjoyed seeing Two Socks and his mother, Moonshadow. They had rejoined my father's herd, bringing Sandstorm and his mares. I guess time had changed their outlook on life. Each had become a vital member of the herd.

My parents were particularly glad to see their grandchildren. That's right! White Heart and I had started our own herd. I sired two beautiful fillies and a handsome young colt. Both White Heart and I were very proud of our little family. After all, they were all brown and white spotted, blue-eyed "Spirit Horses."

And my legend lives on.

From that day forward, thousands of spotted, blue-eyed horses were born on Mother Earth. Many more are destined to arrive. You may already have one gracing your barn or paddock. If you do, take good care of them – love them with all your heart.

If you have not met one of the Spirit Horses, I know you will meet one soon. They are rare and magical creatures, and they are patiently waiting to serve you. And remember me, Sunka Wakan, the Great Spirit Horse. I have gifted you with my most precious possessions-my sacred children. They will forever bring joy, peace, and harmony to the lives of those who love them.

THE END

Sʊɴᴋᴀ Wᴀᴋᴀɴ, the Great Spirit
Horse graces Mother Earth once again. Today,
the legendary blue-eyed spotted horse is better
known as Enough Stuff, a sixteen year old
Tobiano Paint, who presently resides in North
Carolina with his dedicated human friend,
Brooke Hamlin. But many in the Native
community believe Sunka Wakan has returned.

I had the honor of meeting the horse of Plains Indian folklore at the Florida State Horse and Agricultural Festival, held in the fall of 1992. Expecting to acquaint myself with a Paint gelding that I was to show in the Parade of Breeds, I found myself staring at the image of the legend – in the flesh. Enough Stuff gazed at me with his magical blue eyes, and they beckoned me to climb upon his back. From that moment on, my life was forever changed.

For the past nine years, my loyal companion and I have been on an incredible journey. I believe the Great Spirit Horse has chosen me to be his human voice, to educate humanity about my ancestors, and to take him where his magic is most needed.

Enough Stuff has an important mission here on Mother Earth. Many have already felt his powerful spirit and his supernatural gifts reaching out to touch their hearts. He is truly the modern day "Sunka Wakan," for he miraculously brings joy, peace, and harmony to the lives of those he encounters. In time, I am sure he will reveal to humanity the real reason for his return. Until then, I, as well as the rest of the world, will have to be satisfied to marvel at his beauty and wonder about the ancient wisdom displayed in those magnificent blue eyes.

Linda Little Wolf

GLOSSARY

Sunka Wakan (shoon-kah wah-kahn) – phrase for "Great Spirit Horse" in Lakota, translates to "sacred dog"

Mato (mah-toe) – Lakota word for bear

Tanka (tahn-kah) – Plains Indian woman's term for younger sister

Waniyetu (wah-nee-yea-due) – Lakota phrase for winter

Kela (kay-lah) – Lakota word for turtle

Kimi Mila (kee-mee mee-lah) – Lakota word for butterfly

Canyataniwan (chan-yah-tah-nee-wahn) – Plains Indian phrase meaning "swims stick in mouth" and often refers to beaver

Capa (cha-pah) – Plains Indian slang for beaver

Wapiti (wah-pee-tee) – Lakota word for elk

Wambli (wahm-blee) – Lakota word for eagle

Wakinyan (wah-keen-yahn) – word for legendary Thunderbird of Plains Indian folklore

Tate (tah-tay) – Lakota word for wind

Miyaca (mee-yah-cha) – Plains Indian word for "prairie wolf" or coyote

Unktehi (unk-tay-hee) – legendary Plains Indian water monster

Mato Tipi (mah-toe tee-pee) – Lakota phrase for grizzly bear's lodge. Today, Mato Tipi is called Devil's Tower. Located in northeastern Wyoming, it is the largest rock formation of its kind in the United States. Historically, Devil's Tower has played an important role in the lives of millions of people, from prehistoric natives to present-day tourists.

Pilamayaye (pee-lah-mah-yah-yea) – Lakota word for thank you

LINDA LITTLE WOLF, AUTHOR

Born and raised on Long Island, New York, Linda Little Wolf currently resides in Ocala, Florida. She has been an enthusiastic collector of Native American art and artifacts for the past two decades. Ms. Little Wolf enjoys sharing her proud heritage of Cherokee and Lakota Sioux with audiences of all ages. She has rapidly become one of the foremost educators and lecturers on Plains Indian history, culture, folklore, art, and horsemanship.

Her ancestors shared their lives with the horse, and Linda Little Wolf's life is no different. She is often accompanied by her loyal companion and educational partner, a handsome paint horse appropriately named Enough Stuff. He has become an essential part of her lectures, allowing her to demonstrate traditional horsemanship skills while describing the physical and spiritual role that the horse played in the lives of North America's nomadic tribes. Their growing recognition has introduced them to the world of television; they recently appeared in a Ford commercial. Wearing elaborate Plains Indian regalia, this dynamic duo has appeared in schools, colleges, museums, and horse fairs throughout the United States. Ms. Little Wolf has also appeared at equine events in many foreign countries.

Since 1992, Linda Little Wolf has been an active participant in the Florida Horse and Agricultural Festival. In her role as committee member, she has lectured, choreographed, and performed in evening shows and coordinated the Parades of Breeds, the equine performances, and the Youth Pavilion.

Great Spirit Horse is also available as a collectible model from Breyer Animal Creations.

Another book by Linda Little Wolf . . .

VISIONS OF THE BUFFALO PEOPLE

An illustrated activity book exploring the history of the Plains Indians and how the discovery of the horse changed their entire civilization. For more information, visit www.pelicanpub.com.